W9-ANO-594

ACCLAIM FOR
Opium Dreams

"The truths in this interwoven tapestry of lives are painfully close to the bone, yet the poetic vision is leavened with beauty, hope and mercy."   *— Financial Post*

"She writes with sharp beauty and ruthless insight, but, above all, with love. . . . The novel moves beyond blame and despair to a noble vision that has always infused Gibson's work, a vision of human courage, survival and hope."

— Merilyn Simonds, *The Gazette* (Montreal)

"This is a beautiful book. . . . Both wrenching and rewarding to read."   *— The Edmonton Journal*

"The rich prose mirrors the complexity and power of family life, but it also gives the reader a sense of recognition for the personal paths we all must follow."

— Kitchener-Waterloo Record

"Gibson writes in a voice that rings absolutely true. . . ."

— Books in Canada

"Although Margaret Gibson is not yet a household name among Canadian authors, she should be. . . . A powerful writer who skirts the edges of the macabre, Gibson's beautifully, darkly lyrical prose causes the reader to pause, often with astonishment, as her luminous story unfolds. . . ."

— London Free Press

BOOKS BY MARGARET GIBSON

The Butterfly Ward (1976)
Considering Her Condition (1978)
Sweet Poison (1993)
The Fear Room and Other Stories (1996)
Desert Thirst (1997)
Opium Dreams (1997)

Opium Dreams

MARGARET GIBSON

Copyright © 1997 by Margaret Gibson

Published in trade paperback with flaps
by McClelland & Stewart 1997

This trade paperback edition published 1999

All rights reserved. The use of any part of this publication, reproduced,
transmitted in any form or by any means, electronic, mechanical, photocopying, recording, or otherwise, or stored in a retrieval system, without
the prior written consent of the publisher – or, in case of photocopying or
other reprographic copying, a licence from the Canadian Copyright
Licensing Agency – is an infringement of the copyright law.

CANADIAN CATALOGUING IN PUBLICATION DATA

Gibson, Margaret, 1948-
Opium dreams : a novel

ISBN 0-7710-3327-3 (bound)   ISBN 0-7710-3328-1 (pbk.)

I. Title.

PS8563.I325O64   C813'.54   C96-932603-3
PR9199.3.G43O64

We acknowledge the financial support of the Government of Canada
through the Book Publishing Industry Development Program for our
publishing activities. We further acknowledge the support of the
Canada Council for the Arts and the Ontario Arts Council for our
publishing program.

Cover design and photo manipulation: Sari Ginsberg
Cover photographs: Photograph of girl © Kent Miles/Masterfile;
background image "Snow-Covered Aspen Forest" © Lindy
Waidhofer/Creative Stock Photography Agency Ltd.

Typesetting by M&S, Toronto
Printed and bound in Canada

McClelland & Stewart Inc.
The Canadian Publishers
481 University Avenue
Toronto, Ontario
M5G 2E9

1 2 3 4 5   03 02 01 00 99

To Juris Rasa,
who taught me the art of the novel

For Dane Gibson,
the Fly Boy

PROLOGUE

HE WANDERS THE pea-green-coloured halls terrified. He cannot find his room and he knows he left it here somewhere. He must have because he has been nowhere else in – how long? Weeks, months, years? There is no real way of telling, and anyway he supposes it does not matter much, the span of time measured in the circle of a clock hand, a slow-ticking minute frozen in the stale-piss air that hangs like a fog around him or in time measured in light years to the wall of stars. It is all a dreaming now anyway. His mouth, over which a bushy silver moustache perches, hangs a little open, as if waiting to say something. About to say something. Say what? Oh yes. Where is my room?

He moves stiffly, slowly, wire and glass, brittle. He sees the two boys dancing their mops in a Disney Technicolor sweep. He quickly turns in the other direction. He does not like the two boys and their dancing mops and pails. "Naughty, naughty Aggie, naughty little girl, Aggie," he remembers them saying to the woman, Aggie, earlier today. Her long white nightie dragged along the linoleum-tiled floor of her room, and trailing the white lace on her nightie was a string of dark-black feces. "Naughty, naughty Aggie." They chided her and laughed, wagging their fingers. Then finally they came with their mops and pails. He had turned away in shame – and something more. Anyway, maybe his room lies in this other direction.

He wanders down the hall, shuffle, shuffle, dog-paws, and stops in front of a rather innocuous painting of a white-sailed galleon tossed on a blue-green sea. He stands and stares into the picture for a long time. What if his room were in there? Lost in the perimeters of the painting? He wants to find his room. He must find it. He has to pee and, unlike some of them here, he can still go to the bathroom by himself. Hates it when the nurse says, "Mr. Glass, did you go pee-pee today? Number two?"

An old woman, so bent she is a pale, gnarled hundred-year-old tree with spindly feet covered in bumpy purple vines, grips the handrail along the side of the wall and moves (or does not move). He cannot tell. Her movements, like time here, are frozen in her twisted purple branches.

If time were circular like the circulatory system, like the aorta valves, would he end up here in this self-same spot again and again like a Ferris wheel turning and turning forever at a freak carnival lit with deadly bilious green lights? This self-same spot where he watches a woman strapped into a chair and wearing a necklace of mashed-up peas around her soft white throat being fed by one of the aides with a plunger. The plunger is a fat plastic tube in which the mushed-up food, peas, carrots, potatoes, broccoli, spinach, squash, turnip, meat, is propelled through the plunger by means of a thin hard-plastic handle pushed inwards by the nurse or aide.

Usually the attendant grows impatient with the resident's slow eating of the muck and pushes the handle too hard, too fast, and swampy pea-green or poison-yellow food, or the mushed-up meat which he thinks resembles little more than grey shit, dribbles down the resident's chin and here, on this woman, Crystabelle, with her fairy-tale name, has formed a mucky, bilious green-pea necklace around her soft white throat. If time were circular — here in this self-same spot again and again watching Crystabelle (who, it is rumoured, was once a great beauty) being force-fed and wearing a necklace of green peas with no one bothering to wipe it away where once her husband reverently kissed the hollow of that soft white throat — it would be more than someone should have to bear in a lifetime. Or more than one lifetime. Round and round, cruel Ferris wheel. But he's lost something. His car, his car keys, his wallet. No, that was in the Other Time, Before Here. He remembers that much. He is treading water, he is straddling air. Nothing is real any longer. It is all a dreaming now anyway. Now he remembers. He lost his room and he must find it because he has to pee. His bladder presses.

He shuffles in another direction, the air smelling of stale urine and disinfectant. Pale-white balloons, faces like fat white moons with tiny pencil-dot eyeholes behind thick eyeglass lenses, float past him. No one speaks to him. No one has spoken to him since he arrived here except the nurses and the boys when they mop his room with the cream-coloured walls while he pretends to watch the sliding images on the television screen that mean little to him.

He passes through the living-room area, where the floor is in yellow linoleum squares and there is a cracked black leather couch and an overstuffed blue armchair and a green card table set up for the Four Grande Dames who play canasta every afternoon. They are called the Four Grande Dames by the other residents of Sunnydale because the Staff here shows them more respect than they do anyone else, the Four Dames being considered the most "in touch." Nevertheless, under Grande Dame Number Three's chair every afternoon a pond of yellow piss forms, soaking her black crinolines and her white ankle socks, droplets of glistening urine shimmering on her sharply pointed ankle-bones. As a pool of piss has formed now. The two boys take a good hour every afternoon before they mop up the bog of pee. Seeing it, he is only reminded all the more of his own urgency, his own need.

He turns in confusion, round and round like a top, he cannot stop, his blue eyes frightened. To shame himself, to be as the others, strapped into chairs, mouths open as if to speak (and what would they say had they speech?), pink tongues hanging out of black slots of mouths like choice pieces of meat dangling in the window at the corner deli.

Round and round he spins, his white mane of hair flying out and about and – ah God, salvation. For he sees it. His room. Through an open doorway, just two feet away, he cannot mistake it. Hanging over his bed on the smeary cream-coloured wall is a jagged grey sign that bears his

4

flight squadron number in the War, painted in thick white strokes: Flight Squadron Number 517. Of course, how could he not know it – 517 on the jagged grey piece of wood over his bed? This is his room and the bathroom is next to his bed. He races, as much as his broken-man's gait allows, to his room, to his Flight Squadron, Number 517.

Timothy Glass is flying through space. He can no longer sleep. Night after night without sleep. He hears the bombs falling, the black rain, the thunder of the fire, the roiling sky, the thin white fingers of searchlights. He is forgetting things more and more. His reading glasses, his wallet, his handkerchief. There is no one he can tell. He is terrified.

1.

NEVER, NEVER TELL the story of the Glass Family, they said to me. The Sisters Three. Oh, they did not say it flat-out and loud, never like that. Tell it pretty, tell it nice, was what they meant. If I told it otherwise, the cut-glass bowl my sister Rachel was washing in her General Electric avocado-green dishwasher might bear remnants of a soap stain. Leaves might lie heavy, waterlogged, and mouldy on the bottom of swimming pools, or float like curling brown bats' wings in the aqua-blue water. Someone might get drunk one night in the family hot tub on too much wine spritzer. Was that what they were worried about and why they said it in so many ways? Said it in effect only, but once right out loud and screaming over the telephone wire, one Christmas when I thought I'd go insane: *Tell the truth about the Glass Family, Maggie, and you'll be sorry, sorry, sorry as sorry.*

It was said not to tell at family picnics up at the cottage when they spooned homemade potato salad on my paper picnic plate, neat as you please using a silver ice-cream scoop that fashioned the potato salad into a perfect oval mound. A perfect potato salad mound just like my brother-in-law's, Richard's, who then did not say a single word to me or my kid, Reuben, for the entire picnic. We ate side by side, Richard and I, elbows sometimes grazing, tanned skin against tanned skin. We could see each other's teeth masticating the perfect potato salad and throats swallowing down the hamburgers, buns and all, cooked outside on the family barbecue, and we passed the butter politely without a word to garnish the corn on the cob.

The picnic, the eating, and the laughing and talking (talking and laughing save for Reuben – henceforth called The Kid because that is what I've always called him – and me), and the lighting up of cigarettes and sipping of cocktails lasted perhaps two and a half hours when, with an Indian war whoop, my father, Timothy Glass, led all the Glasses running (like lemmings we scattered, following pell-mell after him, bared teeth grim-grinning joy and shivers) into slate-grey cold Gull Lake for a dip.

The gulls flew overhead in white knife Vs.

The Sisters Three said it when they wrote out their names carefully in blue ballpoint pen on strips of white adhesive tape and then taped the strips with their names on them to the pieces of furniture in the Glass House that they wanted when our parents died. I couldn't or wouldn't, besides didn't want, to plaster my name to some bloody bit of furniture before they were even dead or before I was yet twenty. When they weren't dead and I wasn't yet twenty or planning ahead that fucking far.

The Sisters Three said not to tell when they sent notes laced with flowers and dragonflies in the margins and then enclosed photographs of their swimming pools and landscaped gardens and pastel pink and white flagstone patios shaded with blue and green umbrellas over patio tables, but they were afraid to walk down the street The Kid and I lived on. Even in daylight. Abandoned, rusted automobiles littered the sides of that street – rust on the edges of the car doors and underbellies black like a curse and crumbling and curling in deformed shapes, broken glass in green and yellow and brown and clear bits shattered on the rutted road, brittle and sharp as razors, glass from broken wine and whiskey and beer bottles scattered among threads of vomit.

Newspapers twisted and crumpled and stained as old Kotex hurtled down the mean street in the wind that seemed on that street eternal, skimming over the shards of boozy glass that shone in the smudged white sun like silver fish eyes.

They said it when our mother, Clarice Glass, once pretty as her name, went crazy and prayed and sang in the Dominion supermarket and, one day, made French toast, dipping it recipe-proper in egg and milk and then putting it in the electric toaster, and three days later bought breasts, silicone implants, stitched in under her skin like five-pound bags of sugar, her breasts all huffed up and puffed out and heaving, and died five months later at the age of fifty-seven.

Alzheimer's, The Sisters Three said, because somehow

that was more respectable than just going plain out and out nuts, as if one chose craziness like an hors-d'oeuvre from a silver tray, a candy from a tin. (Though craziness is a choice eventually, but a choice one is driven to when the Sanity World can no longer be stood, if one can stand at all any more.) Alzheimer's was not, however, on the coroner's document or indicated in the autopsy performed on my mother. Alzheimer's, Mommy had Alzheimer's, The Sisters Three said, nodding over coffee cups and blueberry muffins, but I know crazy when I see it.

As children they said not to tell in their frilly pastel-coloured frocks, The Three linking arms and skipping down the street, and later when they were grown-up and they went to ski lodges together on holidays and to piano bars in Toronto or Ottawa or Hull to drop shiny coins into Day-Glo pink dishes on the tops of the pianos and drink cocktails stuffed with fruit and turquoise paper umbrellas.

My mother said it too. *Never, never* . . .

But it is my father's admonishments I learned the best, because if any one of the Glass Family burrowed into my heart it was him. Timothy Glass said it as far back as 1950, before I even knew the whole truth of the Glass House, before I knew the truth was him.

At the foot of our street in the suburb of Scarborough were dusty white bluffs with wild yellow grasses growing there like the grasses on a Northern tundra, shimmering golden in waves like wheat in the strong breezes that came off of the lake. Timothy Glass said it when he stood on the edge of the bluffs, one foot dangerously flirting with the crumbling bluff's edge the colour of clay, and looked out across Lake Ontario and saw not Lake Ontario at all but North Africa. He saw North Africa as he shaded his startling blue eyes with one hand, saw the desert swimming like a whole great hot-white rippling ocean before him, the plane gleaming like a silver dart on the tarmac, and he heard the bombs falling by the hundreds, by the thousands, falling and falling, the black rain. The sound of the bombs, he told me later, was a sick, eerie whistling sound, and the thunder filling the air, the whole damn sky, pierced by this high-pitched whistling sigh that sounded like God . . . whispering.

Never, never . . .

But what can they do to me now? Now that I'm older and no longer so susceptible or bewildered when I'm told lie is truth and my truth is lie, my white hair flying across my enormous green eyes like dusty tumbleweeds, like clouds hiding the bafflement, the confusion of – Who am I? What is real? That has already been done, and now what? What could be worse? Scream at me over telephones (one of my ears is half blocked by shattered skull bone anyhow), well, anyway that has been done. Cut me out of wills? Oh well.

If they know that I am Maggie Glass then they know too I do not need many things to be happy. Only magic things.

And I *am* Maggie Glass, and here in my Magic Room with my black cat, Stockings, curled like a comma on the bed, and my sea-blue bottles shaped like Aladdin's lamps and a blue rug laid on the floor and filled with the sun and the moon and the stars embroidered in gold and silver threads and my books in the oak bookcases and the silk Oriental fans with blue butterflies sailing by and the green plants wandering the windowsill and desk, trailing vines and leaves like fingers like hands, and an old-fashioned blue clock, the hands permanently frozen at three a.m., and my desk and my keyboard and white wrought-iron bed, an evergreen tree in a white pot shading the bed and gold antique telephone, lamp, radio, a silk-covered antique pillbox and two fierce wood-carved ornaments I call the Dragon-Birds, heads so evil and twisted, eyes so cruel and sharp, tail feathers so long and curled and vicious they must be prehistoric and at one time have flown over immense valleys, and ashtrays and endless cigarettes sprouting magically, continually, out of a marble cup, a painting of a scrawny black cat on an orange Parisian rooftop yowling at a pink Parisian sky just above Stockings' wicker catbed with the soft curved blue pillow placed on the left side of my bed and you know that that is enough for me.

Because I am *Maggie*.

So there isn't much they can do to me, The Sisters Three, if I tell the truth about the Glass Family now. I'm older now too and truth seems more important the older you get, lines around my eye corners, forty-three this spring, veins more prominent on my hands, and they want to know why please can't I make it pretty, why please can't I make it nice? My mother said it when I was first published: *Why couldn't you make it nice? Why did you have to put sex in it?* Her mouth all crinkled and turned down in a mean-mad witch's frown. And she said, *Write something happy.*

It isn't that none of it was pretty or that none of it was nice, for some of it was, but I have to write the real truth now just so it will stop swimming around and around in my head. I have to make it STOP! To make it BE POLITE! To make it SHUT-UP! once and for all so that I can at last hear myself think, noise-free, clatter-free, shatter-free.

2.

YEARS AGO WHEN I was no longer stupid Maggie Glass, the kid with the funny granny-white hair and eyelashes but grown-poet and some-time short-story writer Maggie Glass, I left Toronto and moved to Kitchener-Waterloo. Packed up The Kid and the one award-winning short-story book and one award-winning poetry book and a couple of suitcases and the guppies and we were gone. Gone in a flash on a Greyhound bus with its sunglass-green windows, leaning back in the seats, stretching our legs out wearily under egg-shaped white night-lights. Only The Kid slept; my eyes were wide and staring like a window sash thrown violently open.

Mile after mile.

It was a terrible thing that caused this sudden leave-taking, a tawdry thing really, like you'd read about in one of those 1950s *True Confession* magazines or *Confidential* magazines, something involving a knife that was such a fine knife, so finely honed it could cut through a roast like butter, like a dream. You could debone a chicken in a minute flat with it, even cut niches into the pale-green arborite countertop in the kitchen if you wanted to.

I sat up all night with that knife, holding it slantwise across my chest so the flat of the blade lay against my beating heart silver in the foyer light, like a fish leaping in sunlight out of water, glinting drops flying from it and blinding. Sat up the whole night. What was left of the night. This was in Toronto.

The Kid was in bed asleep. My bed. He was four and we often piled into bed together to tell dreams, stories, hopes, and make wishes on stars and half-moons, even on dusty curtains if there were no moon or stars, and lay our heads together, his dark curls tangled in with my own wavy long white hair. All furled in a nest we'd sleep, his fists balled up and pressed against my tummy, his sweet cherry lips a little open and breathing song onto my cheek.

I sat like stone all night in an armchair I'd dragged into to the foyer, unmoving save for the flat of the knife blade rising and falling with the beating of my heart. I was breathing in there, I knew, inside the flesh that covered my bones and concealed organs in their bloody sacks. Breath was pumping in-out, I knew in some corner of my brain in a detached way, but what I was, what I was more than flesh and blood and bone and breathing in-out was my own sarcophagus. After I had decided I was the sarcophagus, I could manage to sit there calmly enough through the remainder of the dirty winter night, the snow stained by tramping boots, by breaking, cracking black pools of ice.

There were no stars.

After a time, I could see myself fashioned out of something melted down from metal only, the flat of the knife blade knife blade rising and falling, giving lie to my remaining there until dawn, my toes curled over and white. It was a cold winter night. The knife lay where it had lain all night across my chest, over my still-beating heart like an old companion, the honey-and-white-coloured bone handle gripped in my right hand. I had grown fond of the knife in the night, its closeness, its proximity to me, and the fine sharpness and silver, and was grateful to it for it was all that stood between me and Utter Babbling Madness.

And I had not babbled and I had not gone mad. So maybe that's why it was hard to uncurl my fingers from the animal bone that fashioned the handle of the knife. The fondness. The gratitude. The fingers were stiff as bailing wire, tight as coiled springs. It took a long time to uncurl them. It was only then that the aching in the bones set in. Inferior finger bones, I smirked (suddenly everything seemed a riotous dark joke). I gazed with affection at the animal-bone handle of a knife that could cut roasts like a dream, smooth as melted butter.

I laid the knife on the counter. The counter edge. Close. I washed my face and soaked my aching fingers under the hot-water tap. I woke The Kid and got him breakfast, pink and blue and green Fruit Loops in his Sesame Street bowl with Grover and Big Bird holding hands and capering around the sides of the dish. I filled his round Sesame Street cup with milk and a little dot of tea, a dash of sugar. The Cookie Monster, wild and blue, was eating cookies sloppily on the side of the cup. The Kid wore his red toque at the table and his red idiot mittens and his little yellow underpants. No socks yet. Half dressed. He talked. Wanted toast with peanut butter, please, Mommy, don't burn it. The whole kitchen fell away from me, falling and falling away from me like standing at the top of moving escalator stairs and the stairs rapidly sliding away. I touched the blade of the knife.

Steadied.

Then I made the toast with peanut butter and did not burn it and put another dot of tea and sugar in the Sesame Street cup with the dancing Cookie Monster. "T'anks, Mommy." Black opal eyes bright as candles.

I got him dressed and put his blue and yellow Goofy-dog lunch-box in his hand and walked him out to the lobby of our new, expensive apartment building. We lived on the first floor. We'd moved from the street where the winds raged eternal and forever that The Sisters Three were afraid to walk down even in daylight. I'd written an award-winning book and received a large Canada Council grant and so it was goodbye junkies and juicers and roaming gangs and no heat and often no toilets and armies and *armies* of cockroaches.

We stood side by side and looked out through the wide lobby windows for the yellow school bus. He was in kindergarten at age four. Precocious, my kid, The Kid. His teacher calls him "My little genius."

"Feed the Guys," he said.

"Sure." He meant the guppies. I was thinking of the knife lying on the counter in the kitchen. The yellow school bus pulled into the circular drive of the apartment building. He set down his lunch-box and stood tippy-toe on it and I bent my head for my morning kiss. Pale translucent skin, sweet cherub lips, wild dark curls. Then off he went, his red idiot mittens dangling and swinging like crazy out of the blue sleeves of his winter jacket, and I watched him take the giant step up onto the yellow school bus and waited until I could see the little red toque, the tip of it bobbing up and down until it settled at a window seat. I watched the little red tip of the toque as the bus pulled out of the circular drive, watched it, watched it as the bus moved fast, fast, faster down the road, watched it, watched it even after there was no little red toque tip to be seen any more anywhere.

I walked back down the long hallway with the gold-flecked wallpaper. The hallway was wide and deeply shadowed and I started, held my breath. I imagined ghostly, vaporous hands reaching out of the walls from between the gold flecks on the wallpaper and seizing my ankles, my knees, dragging me down, down, as in that movie *Repulsion* I'd seen years ago by Roman Polanski. Breath held, heart scarcely beating, I ran the last few feet to my door.

I went into the kitchen and touched the shining knife blade. Buddy, friend. And I thought, *He's not my father any more*. Then I phoned the police.

A couple of months later we were on the Greyhound bus, mile after mile on that Greyhound bus that evening, the road a never-ending black winding thread that made you dizzy and night-blind staring at it, stars skimming over the windshield. I thought and thought about the Night of the Knife, seldom getting further than *He's not my father any more*. And *Then I phoned the police.*

There had been a telephone call from my apartment to my parents' house that night at three a.m. Five words I spoke, barely breathed out, the knife trembling in my hand. I said, the words tattooed into cerebral ridges, *Daddy, I've just been raped.* My mother's intake of breath on the other line had been a sharp, hard gasp, disapproving.

After a pause, my father, Timothy Glass, said, *Well, what do you expect me to do about it?*

And although the knife and my three fingers were a bent iron bar moulded around the phone receiver, the last eyelash of my existence, I said calmly enough, in a dead-weight voice, *Nothing, I guess, like always.* And slowly put the receiver back down in the cradle.

Then I moved the armchair into the foyer by the front door, me and the knife and me and the knife and me and the knife sat there the rest of the night.

The Kid woke up. "Sleepy seeds," I said, leaning over him on the grey upholstery of the bus seat. "I'm dusting your sleepy seeds out with fairy dust. Make a wish."

"I wish we had a moat all around this bus and I would build a drawbridge and only I could raise and lower the drawbridge and we'd always be safe." He said this solemnly, his opal eyes filled with dark light.

"Good wish," I responded faintly.

I told him how where we were going we'd see Mennonites, selfless, hard-working people, good people. We'd see them bringing their wares in horse-drawn carriages – produce, milk and cakes and eggs and cheese and vegetables – into the town market on Saturdays. "The women wear long dark dresses and kerchiefs on their heads. The men wear dark suits and white shirts."

"More selfless than the people in Toronto where we live?" The Kid asked, four-year-old eyes shining thirty years.

I had to give a little laugh at that.

"Where will we stay?" He was holding the Guys in the oval fishbowl in his lap.

"Rooms, an apartment, we'll find something."

He sat watching the guppies swim round and round in their bowl, his dark eyes slid when they slid, glided when they glided. I'd never been able to tell how many guppies there were. Seven? Eight? More? Swimming so fast and nowhere with their little black exclamation-mark tails. Watching them was hypnotic. I slept. I dreamt.

In the dream they put a metal hose up me, all the policemen working it, pushing it up, up, higher, higher, and the little detective, John R. Cook, says, "They say no Henry Glass works there. This is for your lies." And with the pain and the frustration I do not tell him again that my father has not used his first name as a moniker since Grade One in school, loathing it, but always uses his second name, Timothy. (John R. Cook phoned my father's place of work after I told him this and asked for Mr. Henry Glass. He was told no one by that name worked there.) Firemen and nurses and doctors come trooping out of a blood-red ambulance, the metal hose plunges deeper into me. Sixteen doctors' hands sailed right up into me impersonally as hands sailing into a breadbox.

I'm as public as a parking lot.

It hurts! It hurts! And no one cares. Unsmiling they mill around me, examining, fingering, this hand plunging in with metal scopes, that hand, another hand. I am not real any more.

Something bursts inside me, a small explosion. There is thunder in my head, and something runs gooey as glucose red rivers down my chest. Blood pools in my belly, floats like a small pond in my belly button, and travels down my inner thigh like menstrual blood. I think it is my heart. But no one notices, the unsmiling faces of nurses and doctors and hands plunging into me goes on and on and on even though my heart has broken and there is a pond of blood in my belly button. . . .

When I wake up fully alive and startled, it is with a silent scream in my throat. Sweating and breathing hard, my white hair matted to my skull like an old woman's hairnet. Some of the dream was real and other parts only mirage; the fog that dreams have, real and dream all mixed in together, a sick mixture like vomit.

It is true that not one nurse or doctor smiled at me all that whole long day or spoke a word to me. It is true too that my housekeeper, Gemma, said, "Sure, you can see the window's been jimmied here," and was completely ignored. The detective ignored my information about Timothy Glass having not used his hated first name, "Henry," since grade school, and was summarily told at my father's office that no Henry Glass worked there.

The rest is dream. (Except for the sixteen impersonal hands and being as public as a parking lot.) After a while counting hands, fingers, probing metal instruments became problematic.

I'd had my first rape dream. It would not be my last.

The first thing we did when we got off the bus in Kitchener, carting our baggage and the guppies' bowl, was to go to the roller-skating rink. We left our suitcases and the Guys with the friendly red-faced man who rented out the roller skates. The Kid had never roller-skated before. Oh but I was fine, cutting rolling figure-eights and The Kid laughing and falling and laughing and falling and laughing some more. Then we got our baggage and the Guys and went to a Tim Horton's across the road for doughnuts and coffee and hot chocolate. An early breakfast. I smoked a cigarette. I looked at the blunt butter knives shining in the sun beside the white napkin holders.

I thought of the Raggedy Ann doll Shadow had torn from my hand and tossed into a far corner of the bedroom. The Kid had given me that doll for Christmas that year. I always slept with her in my hand. I'd left her behind in Toronto. I could never touch her again, and the police did not seem to think it important evidence. I guess I'd been watching the wrong cop shows, which gave misleading information about where one could dust for fingerprints. But maybe cloth can't be dusted for fingerprints. I'm no cop, after all, but Gemma noticed the jimmied window and so did I and the cops did not.

The Kid was eating a double-chocolate doughnut, with chocolate-chip bits. I drank black coffee from a white Tim Horton's mug.

The doll, little Raggedy, just left in the corner she was pitched into. Clarice had said in her long-suffering voice over the telephone before we left that she would tidy up the apartment and send on anything we wanted or needed. Raggedy would not be one of the items.

The next night after the Night of the Knife – my friend – The Kid and I slept at my parents' house. I could not sleep with the light off. Shadow had turned off the hall light when he entered our apartment and plunged the bedroom into blackness. It was Shadow who lay across me. Shadow who put a shadow hand across my mouth, Shadow who pressed a finger into my throat. Shadow breath on my cheek, Shadow lips wet against my ear. Twenty times at my parents' house that night I switched on the light, twenty times Clarice, her face grim as death, marched into the bedroom and turned off the light, and finally she turned on me with such hatred – such hatred! – and hissed, *You were not raped!* Twenty times. How she hated me that night! Hates me still, I thought.

So, left behind is a rag doll I once cherished, loved wholly, for I loved who had given her to me wholly; left behind, too, dusty curtains and worn broadlooms and some lumpy pieces of furniture, plants dying like thin dead grey worms on windowsills.

Left behind two parents. And him. *He's not my father any more.*

It was early spring, the ground was cracking under skeins of ice and snow, muck and the corpses of birds that had henceforth been softly buried and kept warm under glistening white snowdrifts. We watched a cat carry off the corpse of a bird in its mouth, pointy, sharp teeth fashioned into a grin. Dogs' noses sniffing at the corpses. A few weeds had sprung up out of the remnants of dirty snow and melting pools of ice and between the sidewalk cracks. The earth seemed a heaved and breaking thing.

Already the first fly of the year had darted into Tim Horton's and was hovering over sugar bowls and sticky, honeyed doughnuts. Steam rose from cups of coffee thick with cream, cigarette smoke coiled blue into the air.

The earth is a predator, I thought, and slowly, slowly, closed my eyes.

༄

Timothy Glass lies under his bed. He is confused. He is hiding. He is not hiding. "Vroom, vroom!" he says. Something pricks at his mind. The Before Time, before he came here to Sunnydale. They slid him into the narrow fuselage of the plane. It was so narrow you could not turn left or right. Only his head sticking out. Arms pinned to sides. The fuselage – the bombs fell by the hundreds, by the thousands. He rode in the coffin of the plane, the bubble, and could only move one arm. The arm that pulled the lever that released the bombs. He was nineteen years old. There was a narrow space in the coffin of the plane he could see through, the whole world spinning way, way beneath him in dizzying colour, blues, greens, bursts of red and orange flame, sandy colours, spinning, spinning like a crazed kaleidoscope – all those colours – and when a bomb hit its mark he could see the burst of flame and he'd think of what now lay blackened and charred far beneath him.

But no, this was not the plane's fuselage, or the coffin, this narrow thing. It slid slowly into a wall. Now he knew what it was. It was an iron coffin. He was put in it and slid into this wall so slowly, so slowly you thought your heart would burst with the fear, the tightness, your veins would snap like wires and bleed wide open. They slid him into the narrow, dense iron coffin and told him it took pictures of slices of his brain, and after they took him out of it they said he was not all right inside and sent him here. Here – he has been buried alive and brought here – to this place. His mouth opens to release a howling, but he does not make a sound.

Shh! There is no one he can tell. Shh! No one he dares let know how much he can still think. Is capable of thinking. He knows there are nurses on tap-tap-tapping shoes and singing, finger-snapping boys who mop his room and make fun of him, but he pretends not to know and stares at the TV that means nothing to him. Funny-coloured sliding shadows. Shh! Shh! Secrets.

In the War, a man learned how to keep secrets.

"Vroom, vroom."

3.

"HOW DO YOU GET a coffee stain out of a rug," I was
asking Nurse Thatcher at the Halfway House for Epileptics
and Other Shell-Shocked when the letter from one of The
Sisters – Rachel – arrived. We hadn't had much word from
any of them since The Kid and I left all those years ago
when he was four, except that I sent him to Toronto in the
summers to spend time with his grandfather.

We both went back to Toronto for my mother's funeral
when The Kid was nine. It put dry, cold cracks in my heart
to see how small and pale she looked in the grey satin-lined
coffin, as if she'd caught a chill, her once proud and oh-so-
cherished puffed-out breasts all but concealed in the plain
loose blue dress she wore. Her cheeks were highly rouged
like a clown's or an old woman's. But she was not an old
woman. She was fifty-seven. Ice on the ground that day.
We held on to each other, The Kid and I, so that we would
not slip and fall. The Sisters Three and their husbands and

children all formed a long chain like ice skaters doing a dance routine on a rink, the Ice Follies, arms linked.

The ice was so thick and hard on the ground in the cemetery that finally the casket was just left sitting above the ground while the workmen digging the grave with a bright-yellow machine dug as fast and as best they could.

Rachel, and the two sisters younger than I, twins, Lillian and Dinah, each threw a red rose on our mother's casket, but the cold wind coming down through the sparse, leafless trees tore the petals from the roses and they fluttered like crimson drops of blood against the frozen snow. The wind got under your collar, made your teeth and bones chatter. Daddy did not cry. It occurred to me that day that I had never seen my father cry. His face was papery, grey, his mouth tight, controlled.

I was just opening the letter when one of the Eps, Beth-Ann, came lumbering over in her football helmet and said in her gravelly voice that she needed a car ticket. I told her I'd get one for her. Beth-Ann is a nice girl with a sweet, shy sense of humour. She is tall, big-boned and heavy-fleshed with tiny blue eyes, and has so many grand mals a day she has to wear a football helmet. "It just feels bad, is all, just feels bad, is all," she mutters to herself over and over, meaning the fireworks in her brain.

There were others there too that I took care of to support my habit of writing poetry and short stories. Hugh, a tall man, who looked as frail as if he were made of straw. He was once an astronomer down in New Mexico or California, somewhere like that, a brilliant mathematician but the epilepsy had interrupted a lot of that brilliance. One night he had a seizure while he was eating a hard candy, and the Heimlich manoeuvre was administered while a grand mal was in full tilt, his gentle brown eyes wide with terror and confusion and seizure-jolt. We held his flailing edges in our hearts and wanted to roll his tongue neatly back into place like dough with a rolling pin, soothing his electric-sparking brain with our straining fingertips, and then he was laughing, came out of it and was laughing at the absurd jokes we Eps are. Oh, "we Eps," because now I was one too.

I had suffered blows to my head at the age of twenty-seven. My skull was hit so violently again and again that part of it was driven downward and now blocks most of my left earhole. I passed out after the blows and my brain bled and I was never treated for it. I was left with grand mals, petit mals, and fugues too. However, unlike the residents at the Halfway House for Epileptics and Other Shell-Shocked, I didn't live there, I merely worked there to support my addiction to words.

Old Mrs. Bell was one of the Shell-Shocked. She'd had ninety-two shock treatments years ago and now had very little brain left to think with and paced her four-foot strip of worn wine-coloured carpeting, beating her fists together in a thick *slap-thap* sound. Back and forth she went all day, back and forth on those four feet of wine-coloured carpet, her fists beating together over and over again, *slap-thap*, *slap-thap*, her white hair standing up like burning electric coils. You could see the pink of her scalp.

Sometimes she'd say, "Is that the tea wagon I hear coming? Is that the tea wagon?" But the tea wagon laden with dust belonged to another place, the tea wagon with its china cups and rickety, squeaky wheels and silver teapot was in the age of a long-ago Gothic sanatorium far away, where presumably, between cups of tea and vanilla fingers and pink frosted cupcakes, Old Mrs. Bell had had her ninety-two shock treatments wedged in.

I gave Beth-Ann her car ticket and took the letter out to the communal kitchen to read in privacy, passing Paul in his black silk dressing gown with his tiny, trim brown moustache. Paul drew caricatures of mice having fits and swallowing huge, round white Dilantin tablets — their tiny mice throats bulging with pills — or cartoons of the poor mice strapped to shock-treatment tables, their tortured mice eyes shooting out red sparks.

Paul had been there quite a long while, but no one had ever seen him have a seizure. Sometimes he pretended he had gone blind. I nodded to him curtly and, once in the kitchen, I opened the letter knowing it must have been important for any of them to have written at all.

Dear Maggie,

Daddy is sick. They think it may be Alzheimer's. Actually they say that is what it is. Last week Dinah and Lillian and I sat in a neurologist's office on big, fat orange chairs while Daddy was put in this big tube-thing for a CAT scan. He looked frightened and small. Did you know that if you're too fat you can't fit into the tube-thing for the CAT scan, so you can see how narrow and scary it is. It is made of stainless steel and some other material, the neurologist explained to us. Lead, I think he said.

28

Neurologist. We thought it might be a comforting word. Neurologist sounded like the label of someone who might know something. After the CAT scan, Daddy and we three were sitting waiting in the office for the doctor. The neurologist came in, his eyes bright. He said happily, almost jubilantly, hovering by the orange chairs, "Good news! It wasn't a stroke. It's Alzheimer's!"

"Is that good or bad?" Daddy asked.

No one said anything for a moment, then Dinah said, in a voice so soft and breaking that I could have wept, "It's good, Daddy."

Will you come? You have experience working in that halfway house for epileptics, plus being one yourself now. You might be able to help. Please come if you can. Dinah told me about a house she'd seen that you could rent cheap near Gerrard Street. It's important.

Rachel.

Daddy with Alzheimer's. I thought of the damn Great-WhiteCoat fairly dancing with glee around fat orange pumpkins announcing Daddy's Alzheimer's. *Good news! It's Alzheimer's!* Some people are just born assholes. I felt like I had to pee, to void, to explode.

I walked the four streets from the Halfway House to our small flat, three upstairs rooms of a house. I went right to the kitchen and baked a double-layer strawberry cake and cut up crimson strawberries from the Mennonites Market and tucked them into the pink icing. I wanted to give my father something (like a get well card?), but once the cake was finished I saw what a poor gift it made, as if counting him one of the dead already. It would be like people bringing covered casseroles and Bundt cakes back to the bereaved's house after a funeral.

The Kid, in high school then, wasn't home yet. I sat down and ate the whole damn double-layer strawberry-pink cake — stupid idea anyhow — and then I covered my mouth with my hands and screamed and screamed. I hastily wrote down a line on the back of an envelope I thought I might put in a poem one day. *All our lives we ground together sidewise.* . . .

When The Kid came home the house was in darkness save for the light dancing like blue fog out of the television set. I was sitting in front of the TV drinking shots of rye from a kitchen tumbler.

The cake plate lay in the sink, smeared with pink frosting and cake crumbs, the tap morosely dripping fat water drops onto it.

"What's up, Mom?" said The Kid, putting down his books and getting ready to go out riding on his bike. Very outdoor kid, my kid. He loves camping, skiing, canoeing, kayaking. Maybe he'll paddle down the goddamn Amazon after I tell him this, I thought.

"It's Grampops. We've got to go back. He has Alzheimer's."

"But Grampops wears blue jeans and he canoes and can still chop wood with an axe!" The Kid said, his eyes wet. "Oh shit," he said, slowly sitting down on the blue hassock by my feet. "Oh shit." He has always loved his grandfather, whatever differences my father and I may have had. He did not paddle down the Amazon. Instead, later on, after supper he went out into the backyard and began to dig trenches, holes, canyons. When I last looked out the kitchen window at eleven o'clock, the moon lying in the yard like a silver-grey glove, he was digging a hole to China.

That night I lay in bed remembering the past but thinking too we must try to hold him, all his brittle and soft places, the rounded edges still left, no matter what our bitterness. He will move stiffly like a porcelain doll, and if he falls we have to stick all the broken porcelain fingers back on, give him back his porcelain tailbone. How long will he still be able to go to the bathroom by himself? Speak intelligible English? Will he have to have a hose with liquid the colour of apple juice in it running down the inside of his trouser leg that we will have to empty six times a day? Bowel movements?

He must be frightened, so frightened, and I had never seen Daddy frightened before.

Uneasily, I dreamed. I dreamed of Old Mrs. Bell's tea wagon rattling through dim Gothic wards and I saw lying on the tea wagon as it drew closer, among the china teacups and saucers and frosted pink cupcakes, my father laid out like a cadaver covered in thick cobwebs, his blue eyes wide and terrified, Old Mrs. Bell's fists smacking together, *slap-thap*, *slap-thap*, *slap-thap*, *slap-thap*, filling up the whole high-ceilinged Gothic hallway in the dim locked Gothic ward, filling up the whole damn sky, the whole damn, damn inside of my blasted, blasted head.

⌁

On the bus trip returning to Toronto, The Kid holds the Guys in his lap as he did on the trip leaving Toronto. There are two or three less guppies now. Where do they go?

Beth-Ann was very sweet when I left the Halfway House for Epileptics and Other Shell-Shocked. She gave me her football helmet. "Beth-Ann, I can't take this," I told her. "Ah, hell, Mags, you might need it one of these days." And so it is with the gift of Beth-Ann's football helmet, which will no longer guard her but may one day guard me, that I travel back to what I fled.

The Kid doesn't say much except to occasionally mutter, his face reddening, "Grampops wears *blue jeans*." And that is all. Sometimes he speaks to the Guys, dropping bits of the innocuous-looking guppy food into their oval bowl.

We have a cat now, Stockings, just five months old. Two long white stockings run up his front legs, but the rest of him is as black as little black Sambo who ran around and around that palm tree from the tiger. Stockings travels above our heads on the metal racks with the baggage in a cat carrier. Every so often I hear his angry meow. He is cursing this trip and his style of travelling accommodations. Cat curses.

A CD is playing '70s music softly, mile after mile. The girl playing the CD absently chews bubble gum with her mouth wide open. Just to make conversation I say to the woman sitting across from me in the aisle seat, "My poor cat probably doesn't think he's going to live to see the end of this journey. He probably thinks he's going to die."

"Christ, no," says the woman, who can't be more than thirty but with her heavily made-up face looks forty and then some. She is wearing cut-off jeans and a hot-pink sweater. "Animals – because they're like *dumb* animals, right? – can sleep through darn near anything."

"Oh." I turn away. Can't even smoke on these damn Greyhounds any more, even when the company is stupid and driving you crazy. I look at The Kid, who is telling the Guys all about Toronto and how they probably don't remember it much but . . .

I gaze out my window at acre after acre of farmland flooding past in gold. Autumn coming. It is afternoon, we should get into Toronto about three o'clock. The sky is a patchy blue with little white threads and wisps of clouds floating by. Specks of light. Pale-yellow sun rays through the clouds. The sky is only an honest sky at night. I am struck by this thought on this afternoon when the sky looks so jagged and broken. I think I have always thought this.

The night sky with its ungiving curtain of black – with its awesome endlessness. The sky's density and foreverness is the real sky, sometimes lit by a magical blue moon and gems of stars. This is the way the sky is intended to be, filled with mysteries. The Daylit sky is a fraud, fragmented like a broken mirror, shattered by darting, flying birds, bits of leaves and twigs caught in an updraught of wind, pieced like a poorly stitched quilt with cumulus clouds and white tails of clouds or roiling grey clouds, dust motes spinning, distracting the eye, distracting mystery.

It is the night sky filled with Dark and the un-earthly light of the moon and the stars and endless Infinity that is filled with the mystery meant there, Galaxies and God.

I look for a God in that night sky, what with Daddy and all. We are making the turn into Toronto now, and I stretch out the fingers of my right hand to their full length and lay them against the window as if to encompass this city I was born into and fled so long ago and am coming home to now, although home to exactly what I do not know. And it is odd, my fingers seem to grow, stretch and stretch, and the bus window seems to go into a sliding, a stretching like a pulled rubber band, and then the whole bus is stretching rubber-like, elasticized like my ten-foot-long fingers, as if it is telling me, You are home. Home. And you will encompass it, all, all. Whatever may be, whatever, whatever . . .

But when the big Greyhound bus draws into the depot, a wind has come up and is whipping around our ankles, raising dust and small sharp bits of stones.

4.

TIMOTHY GLASS IS TRAVELLING underwater. Black grottos. Glassy caverns. The water is murky and a deep, deep green. It is like looking through green smoke. Here and there he sees openings – flashes of his own life. Someone's life. Like snapshots. Rippling celluloid. Like a sleeping eye opening. A shutter lifted. Then closed again. Timothy is an historian of sorts. A chronicler. He used to keep a stamp collection. A coin collection. Photograph albums bound in leather with wood covers. Timothy remembers he once read that this deep in an ocean, in the ink-black grottos and glassy green caverns, great white blind worms, six feet long, live. The worms are born blind and travel blind all their lives and are only vaguely aware of three things: the ocean water sliding across the surface of their skins, the need for food, and a dim knowing of their own pulsing.

He thinks he is like those blind white worms travelling in darkness and only dimly aware of his pulsing. The hammering of his own heart. Suddenly the great white worms he read of appear in the grotto with him. Does he think it or dream it? It is all a dreaming now anyway. Was it magic? Dream? There is smoke. Green. An eye opening. Blue and smooth as a marble. Like the worms there are long periods of time for Timothy when he is Not-Anything, Not-Dead, Not-Alive, *Born-Not*.

He sleeps. He floats. He cuts through the ocean depths flat as a lily pad sits on pond water. Silky as drifting seaweed. Sometimes there is green smoke; at times the smoke is sheer and filmy as a negligee. At other times the smoke is in great thick balls, huge fat twirling cyclones so that he is peering through smokestacks of green wind.

The eye opening. His life glimpsed. The eyelid lowering. It is tiring, this opening and closing of shutters. He is in so deep, he suspects, so deep (if this is suspicion, thought at all, and Dream-Not) that not even standing high, high up on tiptoe, high, high up. . . . Mother is saying to Kate, "Get my sewing basket, Kate, and I'll sew it back on." And there is his eyebrow, white-blond and soft as a caterpillar, lying on the kitchen table between him and Mother. He got into a fist fight down on Kingswood, a boy knocked his block off and left a shiny red smear of his blood on the snowy cement. Timothy doesn't so much as flinch when Mother puts in the first stitch, although he is sweating with pain, but Father is a stern, taciturn man in a Homburg who carries a silver-knobbed cane, and it would not do to cry. Mother's sewing needle darts just in front of his left eye like a silver sliver of light, caterpillar-silky warm bloody eyebrow is stitched back into its rightful place.

Eyebrow caterpillar warm with blood but stitched in neat as you please, although now its shape will always be that of an awkward triangle unlike the shape of the right eyebrow, a smooth blond arc. The left eyebrow that was so unceremoniously ripped away by a fist (though Timothy had the presence of mind to gather up what eyebrow he could find on the snowy, icy hard pavement) will retain this jagged shape for all of Timothy's life, although it will change in colour from white-blond to blond to light brown to — SNAP — SHUT. . . .

A shutter banged down. Tired, droopy eyelid. Circles like weights beneath those fleshy shutters. A place of sleep so deep now that there are no dreams, no awareness, Not-Anything. Not-Even-Dark. The world skims miles and miles above.

Sometimes it is peaceful here when he gets in this deep. Where there is Not-Anything, there is neither hope nor prayer to hang from. *Hang from the neck until dead.* For a moment a soft, swimming quiet prevails. *Tidal waves bringing messengers.* His eye opening wide.

The Wellington sits on the tarmac gleaming like a bullet in the white sun. He is drinking tea from a billy. The old yellow dogs with the torn ears and ragged tails are lying in the shade of the bomb-bay doors. The orange-eyed wild cats tear at bits of hard-tack with broken claws. An eye closing. Sleep, sleep, a gentle thudding. His own heart. A deep, deep place. The moon rises somewhere in the dark cave of Timothy's sleep. The moon is a golden opal filled with silver threads of stars.

Timothy Glass rises groggily out of the bog of Dark towards the gold opal moon.

Rising . . .

Rising . . .

He is in North Africa standing in the desert with the other Fly Boys watching a black river winding towards them. The ink-dark river bears parrots that are plumed in all the colours of twilight and dusk, perched in little wooden cages, and the dark river bearing the parrots draws closer, closer, closer yet again.

◡

Coma. Daddy's been in the coma a week. Coma? we asked. The Sisters Three and I. How long? Could be — the Great-WhiteCoats extend their fingers, parting their hands to give an expanse of time, a finger clock, a palm calendar, their eyes busy on charts, on each other, on their stethoscopes, the air hanging empty and heavy between their open hands.

Now I sit beside his bed in this hospital room he was transferred to from Sunnydale Nursing Home when he contracted pneumonia then slipped into the coma. He's glad to get away if you ask me. I sit beside this shrunken man who is winter lying on a vast white raft of a bed in a fetal position in a vast white sea of a room. He is winter breath, his snow-white lion's mane of hair tossed back from his forehead and hanging a good inch below his pale earlobes. I wonder if in the middle of the night he sits up in bed, suddenly lucid, and shouts "Row! Row!" commands issued across a white and chrome sea. Frosted breath and thin as tissue. How can I blame him still? How can I not gather him up in my arms and whisper, "Daddy." But instead I want to see what truths are left in him. I want to lean over him and tap on his ear gently and whisper into it – into him – *All our lives we ground together sidewise. You and I . . .*

If he could hear (and who is to say that he can hear nothing down there in whatever rooms he inhabits?), he would know it was me, Maggie. Number-Two Daughter, the Dreamer. He would know. It would not be cruel to say it. We need reconciliation.

The Kid and I arrived here seven and a half months ago when Daddy was in Sunnydale Nursing Home. Strip parlours and go-go girls with G-strings up the centre of the crack in their asses one street up from the Home, boozy, sad-looking, dusty-windowed little bars, ancient movie theatres, huge gleaming-white drugstores that sell clothing and food as well as drugs.

"There were clues," says my sister Dinah, busily arranging flowers on the sills of the hospital windows. "We just didn't see them." Babies' breath, irises, lilies, a sprig of mint, violets. "The way he kept losing his car keys. The way he lost the *car*. And the way he would get all wound up in the telephone cord, round and round it would go all about him until he was *virtually trapped* in the telephone wire. Oh, Maggie, you know how many computers I've got now?"

Dinah's kids are playing out in the hospital corridor near a big red and white Coke machine and, ludicrously, there is a television turned on in the room. "The Young and the Restless." I'm not listening to any of it, though, to the kids giggling or Dinah prattling on about her computers and work or the soap opera on the TV. I'm thinking, Of course

39

there were clues. I should have guessed, but his behaviour was often odd.

A clue: The time The Kid and I were living in some squalid slum on the street everyone was afraid to visit and Daddy bought us a new mattress for our double bed, but it was a single mattress for a twin bed. "They don't make the other kind any more," he informed us. We had to sleep on the floor for months. Months later he again clenched his teeth and came out to the wilds of our street to our squalid slum with a double-sized mattress for our double bed, announcing like a conqueror that he'd gotten the last double-bed-sized mattress left in Toronto.

There was another time too that was odd. A birthday party he gave for The Kid when he invited only two other boys, boys The Kid scarcely knew, and he had arranged no games or party favours. He served the children one hot dog apiece for the party food. There was no cake, no ice cream. That was not like my father to be so callous or unknowing about a boy's birthday. And certainly not The Kid's.

The way he started buying lard in bulk in big plastic buckets instead of butter or even margarine, because it was cheaper, and Daddy is by no means a poor man.

On the hospital sheet that lies over his right arm, the sheet as white as a crystallized snowdrift, there is a drop of blood that forms a perfect scarlet tear. Some nurse careless with the IV needle recklessly plunged it into his poor tortured purpled vein.

I stand for several minutes gazing at the drop of blood, the scarlet tear. He is in there somewhere and he is alive and therefore — knows? This damn Hieronymus Bosch of a disease, a Salvador Dali canvas done up in smears of blood and blanks and edges of worlds and lopsided clocks with frozen hands and vast black nights filled with razor blades instead of stars.

It is then tears well up in my eyes, childhood's end lies in this bed with the dying man. Mine. His. And some of it was good, so good, and even when it was bad it was always magical. I grieve. I grieve over this man adrift on the great white raft floating among tubes and chrome-raised bed-sides, a brown rubber sheet beneath him and between what high dark cliffs, through what frothing, turbulent seas of Alzheimer's he drifts I can only imagine. Sunlight comes through the wide windows white-frosted as fluorescent lighting and Daddy sailing, sailing . . . away.

Doctors have told me that a coma is a sleep deeper than the deepest sleep of ordinary natural sleep.

It makes me think of all the sleeps. Where do I, for example, disappear to when having a fugue? One's brain remains active and functioning but simply without you. So where do you go? Not into a box. There are no cardboard sides, no cardboard top or bottom. Not into blackness, there is no black. But one's brain is simply gone from you, acting on its own. Then where am I? My father sailing, sailing out to almost anywhere — a primeval sea? Sailing . . . even *beyond*.

∽

When I get home to the sandy-brick townhouse The Kid and I rent, with its small yard and garden, I make coffee in the percolator. The percolator and this nice (though small) two-storey house, which sits in the middle of a park with nine other townhouses, are made possible for us by another award (cash) and a grant I received and my pay from the Halfway House for Epileptics and Other Shell-Shocked. Plus the few piddling little bits of royalties trickling in from the poetry and two books of short stories.

We open our front door to our gated yard, and beyond our gate lies the park, resplendent with weeping willow trees, poplars, and tall maples inhabited by birds and squirrels and mice and raccoons, and garter snakes that coil blissfully in the sun in our small gardens and bake on the hot white patio stones.

Gerrard Street is less than two blocks south, with its Indian markets, saris sweeping the streets in whispers, corn with hot pepper roasted on spits on the sidewalks in the summers, and ten-pound bags of rice and white beans for sale on every street corner, plus dozens of little hole-in-the-wall restaurants with red velvet curtains, spicy foods, exotic beer, and sweet rice cakes and tiny candies in rainbow colours.

There are people with skin the colour of rich dark chocolate and Chinese clerks in smoke shops who read newspapers right to left and smoke thin cigarillos. There are doughnut shops everywhere, with slippery neon signs and the sad, limp tinsel that the doughnut-shop owners string up every Christmas while Christmas music pours from staticky AM/FM radios.

The Kid has left a note saying he is out with the Chinese Boys. He runs in a pack of ten Chinese boys and one Pakistani boy. It makes me smile to see all those yellow skins and one walnut-stained skin on their bikes with The Kid's pale-white translucent face right in the middle, pedalling for all he's worth.

He's learned some Chinese but only the curse words.

I smile. No, no, it was not a mistake to come back here. His grandfather is dying. My father is dying.

Now I go up the long staircase, taking with me a glass of rye to my Magic Room where Stockings lies blissfully fast asleep, all four legs sticking up in the air as if rigor mortis has set in. When I first spied him sleeping like that I thought for sure he was dead and tried to commence mouth-to-mouth resuscitation into his yowling pink cat mouth. I kiss his tail, I nuzzle his cool black nose and dish out his Whiskas cat food and 9 Lives kibble in two plastic TV-dinner dishes beside the evergreen tree. Here in the Magic Room we do not necessarily eat oranges from Ceylon or drink tea from China.

I look through my shuttered windows. One shutter open. The auras smoke. They sparkle like Roman candles. Ruby red, emerald green, silver, gold shooting stars. The auras say that he is in there somewhere and that he is alive and that he knows. Sometimes at night when I go to bed and The Kid isn't home yet and my eyes ache, whole auras of red, smoking haloes fill my eyeholes, but once The Kid is in the door the auras calm into wispy white tails of shooting stars, whispering, whispering, *He is in there somewhere and he knows and is . . . alive . . . alive. . . .*

I sit at my desk among my blue-green glass bottles and my Dragon-Birds, and the photographs fall from the ancient albums, the spines of the albums so weathered and weak that they creak and snap. I have come up here to – discover. Find out who the Glasses were. Most particularly him. If there was a past I could understand, I could understand his failure to never stand up for me, even once. Photographs by the hundreds spill out of the ancient albums like autumn leaves once waxed and pressed lovingly into a scrapbook. Or urgent messages to be read from a long-lost old mailbag and translated into poems.

My father, the chronicler, the historian.

There are women in tiny two-by-four black-and-white photographs with their hair pinned up and parasols and high-buttoned shoes; more recent photographs of women with Vivien Leigh hair and sling-back shoes and padded shoulders and kerchiefs wrapped gaily around their necks. A photograph of an uncle I never met, my father's older brother, older by nineteen years, dead now, standing on a white-iced winter beach by "The One Hundred Steps" with his dog named Squeak. He is smiling and wearing a coat with a black fur collar. He is tall and handsome with a noble nose and strong chin. Clear eyes.

There are cars high as houses with running boards.

A photograph of a fat tabby cat cleaning its paws luxuriously in the sunlight on my grandmother's wide verandah.

A snapshot of my Aunt Kate dressed for a ball at the private girls' school she attended, wearing a white powdered wig with curls. Aunt Kate was a real beauty with her deep-blue eyes and slender figure and beautiful hands.

Fly Boys tumble out everywhere. Fly Boys suiting up. Fly Boys with their arms slung around one another, smiling straight into the sun, the plane a narrow silver letter-opener behind them. The plane that will take them Up in a few hours. Parrots perched in an arc on the nose of the Wellington. Mascot monkeys cleaning lice from their masters' hair, grooming them. Wild-eyed cats cleaning their paws and faces and rumps and balls with serious luxurious intensity, Fly Boys sitting nearby and tossing them bits of bully beef. Fly Boys with bare-naked asses sliding into skivvies. Fly Boys leaning against nothing but sheer air, as if weightless, and smoking hand-rolled cigarettes. Parachutes unfurled and lying like big white puffs of whipped cream or clouds in the desert which have fallen to Earth.

And one tiny photograph of King Street in Toronto in winter. You can make out the words "King Street" clearly on the sign. And just off on one side of King Street is a makeshift office desk with a white banner over it, a sheet flapping in winter wind, which says on it in black letters, RECRUITING CENTRE. A few people, so blurred and grey and white they appear more like ghosts than people, can be seen walking arm in arm down the snowy sidewalks. I turn the tiny photograph over. Ever the historian. Daddy has written in black ink in his clear, strong elegant hand, *War – 1940*.

5.

TIMOTHY IS THINKING of the bat caves but he isn't sure why — weren't the bat caves after the War? And surely this is before the War, because here sits Clarice Magraw, pretty as a picture in her little fox-fur tails and red boots and her blue poetry book. Timothy has floated through a door in the buried swimming-green sea. The murk and glassy caverns have parted. The autumn sky above them is a perfect baby blue. "Like my girlfriend's nephew's little Jackie's baby booties," Clarice says and smiles.

He is telling Clarice, seventeen-year-old Clarice Magraw, that he is in love with her, and to prove it he draws out a rust-red poetry book of his own from his back pocket. In it is a poem entitled "When Martha Goes Walking in Her Silk Stockings." He says she is like Martha, that beautiful, that enchanting, when she goes out walking past his verandah on an autumn or spring day in her silk stockings. Timothy sleeps on the verandah of his house in clement weather, and every time he spies Clarice swaying those lovely hips, her legs in the silk stockings, he whistles through the verandah window. It used to embarrass her. Now, frankly, it pleases her to no end.

The silk of her stockings is as soft as gossamer, as butterfly wings, and they make a soft whispering sound, he says.

Clarice doesn't quite know what to say and all the more because she sees that Timothy has clipped this poem about Martha and her silk stockings from a magazine and pasted it into his poetry book. This is serious. They've been dating since Grade Nine and have known one another since Timothy was five years old, but this seems rather more serious. Her silk stockings. He said they made a whispery sound.

She delves into her leather shoulder bag and again takes out her little blue book of poetry. She wants to show him something. And she does. Little Latin translations in the margins. She tells him she loves poetry too and wants to learn Latin translations. More of them. She knows some French as well, she adds, ducking her head shyly, hiding her pretty rouged face behind her long curly chestnut-brown hair.

Does he see he's getting a woman who wants to go somewhere in life?

And maybe, maybe, he sees she has something more, more than other girls, pizzazz, magic, something special, because he takes a little blue velvet box from his pocket and opens it and inside is a perfect tiny shiny silver bee of an engagement ring. He's joining up tomorrow and will she wait for him? The ring is small, beautiful.

"These Latin translations and French – "

"Hell," Timothy says, grandiosely throwing one arm boldly around her shoulder, "I'll buy you French champagne on our wedding night."

She tries the ring on and it sits, a glittering perfect bee, on her ring finger and she *does* love him, she thinks she always has. It looks splendid. He thinks she is beautiful. He tells her that all the time, and yet shows the greatest respect. He never tries to paw her, only kissing and hugging and hand-holding. Not like *some* men. She closes her little blue poetry book with its messages in Latin scrawled inside.

"But you're going? You're really going?"

"Hell yes. All the guys are. Bertie just over on Windemere signed up yesterday and my best buddy, Andy Cawswell, is going down tomorrow. I'm going with him. All the guys are going. It's our duty. For Country and God and Queen. It's England now. Winnie said. We listened to Winnie last night on the wireless in the front parlour, Mother and Father and Kate and Budd and I, and Winnie said, England now. Mother wept. She balled up her handkerchief and wept into her teacup in her lap. She said, 'Winnie will save us! Winnie will win!'"

"I'll write. I'll write every day. I'll knit scarves and sweaters and send you socks and cigarettes. I'll wait for you. I won't die even though every day, every second of every day, I'll be scared to death for you. I'll save tinfoil."

Timothy calls her dear and his sweet, sweet sweetheart and leans over her and kisses her on the eyelids.

Sweet, sweet open door buried in the deep that I have floated into . . .

But time is a trick down here in this buried place where you can be Not-Anything, Not-Dead, Not-Alive, Born-Not. As if through an inky-green haze (and it seems very long ago) Timothy remembers lying in a bed (long ago? not?) in a horrible place with smeary cream-coloured walls and halls that smelled of stale piss and soap, staring hour after hour at the cracks in the ceiling. He wondered if they were narrow entranceways into another world. A parallel universe or an upside-down world where chairs and tables and people's feet were all bolted to the ceiling.

He remembers staring at threads in the blankets, following the threads with his eyes, his fingers fingering the textures of the threads, thinking they might be lifelines that a gypsy with a cup of tea and green tea leaves and a murky glass ball could read. Lifelines like those seen in the palms of hands when hands were young and strong and could do things. This makes him very sad for, suddenly – and for the first time since he floated down here (wherever *here* might actually be) – he realizes his hands are no longer young and strong and can't do things. Or can they? Just a few moments ago his hands were young and strong and on sweet Clarice's shoulders. But where are his hands now? He cannot see them. He can see nothing but green murk and shadow.

He is the worm. That is what it is to live so deep that not even air skims over you.

Mother said, "Things always seem worse in the dark, and if you think that way long enough worst may come." Mother was wise, Mother was beautiful; she had violet eyes

49

and long white hair that fell to her waist. Seems he knew someone else with long white hair, but he cannot recall who.

But too long he has been in the Dark and blind. Worst just came. He has floated without will into another opening and he is five years old and wearing his little blue velvet winter coat, Christmas soon, and galoshes and blue mittens and his little blue velvet hat with the earflaps. Father has put on his Homburg and his black coat with the deep black pockets and fetched his silver-knobbed cane and soft-brown kid gloves. Father says he is taking him somewhere. There is something he wants him to see.

They travel on the streetcar for many, many miles, almost to the outskirts of Toronto. They walk in silence along the snow-packed sidewalks. Timothy's galoshes make squeaking sounds against the snow. Father does not hold his hand, but then he seldom does. Finally, they stop in front of a brutish brown-brick building with army-green-coloured doors and small high windows.

Father gestures him inside.

Inside, he sees things that are like children. Children made out of funny rags and shapes and only half stitched together, half finished. There are children with heads the size of watermelons and children with no feet or webbed feet like ducks and children with flippers instead of arms and legs, one-eyed children, a child with no nose, only a hole where a nose should be. Green snot drenches out from the hole. Some of the rag children are tied into chairs. Others are restrained by straps in crib-beds. There is a boy with a bilious hump on his back. His thin undershirt cannot conceal the yellow sheen of his hump, the poisons spilling out. Children with huge stitched tongues lolling out of their heads. Children crying screaming rocking banging their heads beating their faces with their own fists.

Timothy and his father travel down dim green hallway after dim green hallway with high dark windows covered in mesh. Another child with no nose drools on Timothy's pretty blue velvet coat. Father makes Timothy shake hands with the boy but the boy's hand doesn't fit right. The child's whole hand is no bigger than a half-dollar. The moaning the howling the tears the misery the feces smeared on bed-clothes on walls on faces. Hallway after hallway of crib-beds crammed with mewling, howling things.

When they leave the Home for the Crippled and Retarded Children, Timothy's eyes stinging from the wind, stinging from a darker secret knowledge, Father adjusts his Homburg and twirls his silver-knobbed cane and says, "Never let me hear you complain about what you get for Christmas."

Timothy drifts in a tunnel of time, away from high meshed windows that let in no light or air, into a placid pool of warm, warm green. It covers him like a blanket, and he thinks (Is this thought? Am I mad? Dead? Is this a Dream Walking?) that it was years before he realized that his father did not intend to put him in the Home for the Crippled and Retarded Children if he were bad but only that Timothy should realize what a lucky, fortunate boy he was and to never, never complain. For years he was terrified that he would be sent away to the Home if he were bad, where he would be tied down in a crib-bed in a dim green hall with half-finished things stitched from rags that looked like children and howled, where he would lie under high dark windows forever.

Timothy wonders if his father can come back to this deep place, in this Land of Not, and he hopes that he cannot. The Land of Not. The Place of Not. He could laugh aloud. He has finally found a name for this peculiar dimension.

Timothy never did complain, not once.

The word *monster* coils in Timothy's unravelling brain like white smoke.

6.

I SIT WITH my glass of rye. The photographs spill onto
the floor, onto the rug of stars and suns and moons, like a
montage. Like clues. Maps. The Kid is studying the drawing
of maps in school. He would like to be a mapmaker. Right
now he is in his room listening to Whitesnake full blast. The
walls shake with it, the bathroom taps sing and ring with the
pulsing beats. Maybe I could ask him to draw me a map of
his grandfather's life, the eddies and cliffs, the clouds high,
high up and nearer to God that consumed him, the mountains he climbed, the valleys of the mind he fell into, the
desert he slept in and flew over and fought in. Maybe I could
ask him to draw on the map a little stick figure of the boy
that became the man.

Or I could ask The Kid to map my auras, which sail
under my closed eyelids like shooting stars, comets trailing
fiery-red tails. About the auras The Kid just laughs and says,
"Ah, Mom, those are just your damn meteors falling to

Earth and knocking your brains in, *splat-flat*, putting cinders in your skull."

Maybe.

I tip the rye bottle on my desk into the kitchen glass. I am a plain drinker. When I drink I make no games of it. The pictures of my father as a small boy have told me he was a shy boy with a sweet, sensitive face. Frail. Brilliant blue eyes shine forth from the one photograph my grandmother had an artist paint in the colours of his features. Eyes, skin colouring, hair, roses in his cheeks. His father smiles in not one picture. Someone mentioned that Daddy's father looked like Buster Keaton when I showed them a photograph. There is a certain likeness. My grandmother smiles, always showing her perfect tiny teeth, as she carries tea trays with a silver tea service, plates of baked scones with raisins in them, her beautiful snow-white hair piled in a roll on top of her head. I loved my grandmother. I believe she loved me.

Dinah said there must have been clues. And there were. Doctors talk of genetics, of links in blood cells, genes, heredity, DNA like threads hooked and running together to make a single stocking.

My grandmother, my father's mother, did not let down her long white hair and let it float wild and wander barefoot in winter moonlight, her hair the moonlight or the moonlight her hair, who could tell which, and babble crazy things and die in an asylum. My grandfather in his stiff Homburg hat, with his stiff, unsmiling mouth, died of sternness; it got into his veins, filled and tightened his arteries, and he had a stroke. My grandmother died in my Aunt Kate's bed at my Aunt Kate's house at the age of eighty-six, the fingers of one hand still warm on the Irish linen, my father holding her other hand.

On Clarice's side, her mother had no time to grow old and court dementia praecox but died seven months' pregnant after she caught pneumonia; died when Clarice-was-only-six, we were told every time Clarice lined up our teacups on our placemats.

Similarly, her father had little time to grow old and hand his brain over to the unwindings of Alzheimer's but died when my mother was nineteen years old. He was sitting in his armchair as he did every night after supper, the newspaper full of War, though he always loved to read "Mutt and Jeff" first. My mother was climbing the staircase to her room when she heard a sick, flat thump.

"Daddy?"

When she ran back down the stairs and to him he was on the floor, one arm flung across Mutt and Jeff's capers, his pulse-place already quieted, stopped-up-flat-dead, the kisses she loved to shower on his bald head after supper still there in fluted red lipstick.

A great uncle fought in the First World War and told us of no man's land and sinking beneath the greyish-yellow muck with only his bayonet tip peeping above (that was how he was saved – a comrade saw the tip of the bayonet and grabbed it, pulling the sharp silver tip upwards and Nunc came up with it covered in muck and gasping but alive). He died of cancer in his late seventies. He brought us chocolate bars and *National Geographic* magazine every Sunday when he came to help Daddy in the gardens and he stayed every Sunday for dinner. He drank brandy out of a tiny liqueur glass, which shone so that it seemed gold in the rosy autumn twilights. The chocolate bars were packed with nuts and fruit, and he gave each of us girls a brand-new shiny silver dollar every Christmas.

We called him Nunc because when we were small children we could not pronounce "uncle" so we called him Nunc or Nuncy, and even when we grew older and right up to the time of his death that was all we ever did call him. I remember I cried when he died. He did not take to shambling into strangers' homes in his worn bedroom slippers, babbling War stories from the first Big One, or talk about the days when he went fishing as a boy up at Lake Scugog. He died a terrible, painful death on cold white sheets in a cold white hospital room.

There were other uncles too, of course, some living, some dead. But those that were dead had died in the War and those that were living came at Christmas with their burned-off ears or maimed feet and sundry scars and stood in cardigans in front of the fireplace, the fire lit and licking orange dancing flames, drinking scotch and water and eating salted nuts and talking of the War.

The War, the War, it was everything when I was a child.

I have thought of the great-grandmothers and great-grandfathers there may have been and the great-uncles and great-aunts, but their histories are lost to me in a land of green and poetry and wee folk and War, in Ireland from which both sets of my parents' parents came.

There are things to remember, Lillian advised me in a phone call from Ottawa. Throw out all your aluminum pots and pans. Don't live near a lake with a lot of aluminum in it, and, if you do, don't drink the water. Boil it first. Cut down on red meat.

"Don't use aerosol containers," Rachel said in a later phone call from Ottawa. "Throw them all out, cleaners, cans of hairspray, everything. And, whatever you do, if you ever do find a guy, for godssake get a pre-nuptial agreement."

My sisters Rachel and Lillian both live in Ottawa and have husbands and children there, three apiece. It is Dinah and now I who live in Toronto. Dinah with her husband and two children and me with no husband and The Kid. We seldom see each other, only at family gatherings, although she lives only one neighbourhood away. We have never once had coffee together alone at each other's homes. They were afraid to walk, or drive, down that ruined, rumpled street, even in daylight hours.

Auras float in my eyeholes in dusky haloes. *He is in there somewhere . . . alive . . . alive. . . . The Fly Boy is taking a new flight now.* The auras float in golden-red haloes. Just shut the fuck up! Too much rye maybe and not enough Valproic Acid. Cinders in my skull, The Kid would say.

Once, thousands of stones fell in Ontario back in 1952 and the sky lit up at sunset like the Fourth of July in eerie colours. Hundreds and hundreds of burning rocks fell to the earth. Terrified Canadians thought that the United States had been bombed by the Russians, or that Armageddon, the Day of Judgement, the End of the World had finally come. (Will the crazies and the cripples and the animals be spared?) For miles and miles around, little dust storms were raised by the rocks that fell from the sky.

It was meteors, meteorites, small bits of planets hurtling to Earth. "You and your epilepsy and auras caving in your brain, meteors filling it up with dust and cinders, giving you fugues," The Kid laughs.

Maybe. But I still don't want to remember how my father's hands shook in the nursing home clinging to a bit of Kleenex, wringing it to shreds in his trembling hands. And sad, sad, Flight Squadron Number 517 painted in thick white strokes on the jagged piece of grey wood hanging on the wall above his narrow bed. His roommate had one leg eaten away into an angry purple by some disease and was always stealing the chocolates I brought Daddy, which made Daddy cry.

For a while we attempted to have Daddy here. A very short while. Dinah brought him in her van in the early afternoon. He wore his golfing cap and a green cardigan and blue jogging trousers. He carried a single suitcase. He sat stiff-limbed on the living-room couch for a moment and declined an offer of tea. The Kid grinned foolishly at his grandfather – The Kid lost. Daddy was made of porcelain, something strung out of wires and planks, a marionette. Surely no human made of flesh and blood and bone, chromosomes linked in neat chains, could walk so stiffly, sit so fragilely, legs bent like wires, chin tilted defiantly into an invisible threatening wind. He'd take a Kleenex from his cardigan sleeve and blow his nose once in it and then begin the brittle, slow walk to the kitchen where he deposited the Kleenex into the wastebasket. Then the porcelain-and-wire-doll journey back, chin tilted into the threatening winds. Tornadoes? Cyclones? A great force bearing down on him and he was fighting it for all he was worth, taking it on the chin like a man. Then he'd extract another Kleenex from the wrist of his green cardigan and blow his nose in it once and then the slow journey to the kitchen wastebasket would begin again.

This went on all afternoon.

I went to great trouble to make a good dinner, as I am not the best of cooks. Roast chicken, steamed peas, dinner rolls, and baked potatoes, strawberry ice cream for desert. He ate none of it. I scraped his plate into the garbage. Steam from the tea kettle mingled with the wet on my face.

"Show Grampops where he sleeps," I told The Kid.

"O-kee-doke." The Kid led his grandfather on his stiff-wired walk up the stairs. "You sleep on this bed, Grampops," I heard The Kid say and heard him pat the bed for his grandfather. Springs creaked. I heard my father say to him, "Well, dear, you sure are the best-looking one of the bunch of the kids. And the smartest." I was gathering porcelain fingers, glass feet and toenails, a wire knuckle.

"Gee thanks, Grampops," I heard The Kid say.

Later, when The Kid and I had been sitting downstairs watching TV for a while, The Kid went upstairs to use the bathroom and the next thing I heard was:

"Where the hell is Grampops?" And then, "Holy shit!"

Frantically I looked all through the small house. "Get on your bike and go out looking for him!" I commanded.

"Holy shit," said The Kid again, leaning low into his bike like a professional racer built for speed. "Grampops! Gram-pops!" I heard his voice calling eerily out into purple falling dusk as he rode off on his bike on his search.

He found his grandfather four blocks up the street walking at a swift pace. His grandfather blinked at him, his once-vivid blue eyes gone a pale almost-transparent blue. "I want to go back," he said.

"Go back?" asked The Kid. "Go back to where? To the nursing home?"

"Right-o."

The Kid said later it looked like he was going to cry.

I called Dinah and she came over wearing her little business blue hat and blue business skirt, carrying her cellular phone with her two children in tow who chased Stockings around and around until he hid on top of the dinette cabinet. I scarcely had to pack Daddy's bag save to fold a white hand-kerchief into it and hand him his grey golfing cap, which he had set carefully on the edge of his pillow. He hadn't even opened his bag. I felt – nothing. Not yet.

Not until I watched him walk out of our tidy, gated yard, Dinah leading him by one green cardigan sleeve, Kleenex trailing, her two kids skipping behind, and I watched him walk down the little stone laneway between our gate and the park, his white-haired head bent, watched him walk farther and farther away, the porcelain doll whose edges I said I must hold, whose broken porcelain fingers I said I would glue back on, and I had done none of these things, not really. He would rather go back to a nursing home that smelled of piss and disinfectant than stay with me, and I watched him, watched him disappearing, disap-pearing, disappearing. . . .

All our lives we ground together sidewise. . . .

7.

A SHUTTERED EYE. Not-Anything, Not-Dead, Not-Alive. His brain tortured and shrinking is the snail shell tucked away in his near motionless body. He breathes in-out. Sometimes his upper lip draws back. He does not see the flowers so carefully arranged on the hospital windowsills. Nor does he feel the catheter being pulled out from his penis and drained, a new one put in. These ignobilities he had to suffer at the nursing home before the coma visited him, had to suffer though he had a brain but no right to protest or use it. He will remember later how he winced when the nurses said, "Have you pee-peed?" or "Poopy yet today, Mr. Glass?" It is safer here in this territory where there are long blank empty streaks and endless green passageways and no sound. The Land of Not. A Place of Not.

But such a curious realm these depths of inner space. An eye opening and he is eating figs and goat meat and eggs with the Arabs, the desert sun a huge orb of shimmering white heat causing the sky to glow white and hot-hot, and later he and the other Fly Boys smoke the opium their Arab hosts so kindly offer. He sees the camels. The Fly Boys have to use the camels, but they hate the camels. They are difficult to get to stand or move at all and they spit into the Fly Boys' astonished eyes. But Timothy likes the camels' eyes – big, wet brown doe eyes that belie the camels' mean-spiritedness. The gobs of spit they are more than happy to aim smack-dab at the disgusted, faintly repulsed Fly Boys.

Timothy is shivering. Night has fallen, and it grows cold in the desert at night. He and the other Fly Boys have bedded down. They sleep huddled together, knees drawn up into the backs of knees, cuddling to keep warm, curved into one another like spoons, like small frightened children. The opium gives them strange dreams. Gives them waking walking dreams and slumbering dreams both. It makes them dream of strange beguiling women, with hair as soft as shadows and silk, and sirens' eyes, who stroke their damp foreheads as they dream.

They dream too of vast starless nights, nights without a single star or moon for light and nothing but black wind and black sky reaching on forever.

When Timothy awakes, he is shivering. The desert sun not yet risen in the cold morning. He is shivering from the sweat, the night, the opium dreams. The Fly Boys do not like the opium night-dreams. To dream of the seductive women with the sirens' eyes and hair like shadows and silk makes them feel like they are betraying their sweethearts back home to whom they are pinned and who are after all knitting them socks and scarves and sending them cigarettes and writing them letters every day. Mothers are putting stars in windows and weeping. The dreams guilt-fill them.

Nor do they like to dream of the endless black nights with the howling winds. It is too close to what they have to face daily. Eternity. Going Up. Nearer to Dark and God. Timothy rides in the belly of the plane. He is the bombardier. The belly of the plane is called the coffin. The coffin and nearer to God and Dark and His whisperings. And never knowing. Never knowing about the coming back; if you will. Coming back after a night raid there are the dawn patrols, thin white fingers of searchlights crawling the skies.

Timothy smokes the opium and shivers. His cold white bones clatter in the purple oncoming dawn. When he curls into sleep again against another Fly Boy, he dreams of a two-headed bird with the scaly green tail of a mermaid, who flies straight into the pupil of his bright blue eye, hissing and cawing and plucking his eye out and eating it down like a rare, exquisite blue olive, the bird's oil-black beak snap-shut. Timothy shudders under the disappearing white desert moon floating in the purpling sky like cold glass and he dreams on and on.

He dreams wide-awake of rowing across the River Styx with Charon the Dog-Face (who, he remembers from a high-school text, was Greek). The River Styx smells like the belly of rotting corpses split open with a knife. Later, when Timothy blinks, even as the desert morning fades towards blistering noon and the dancing monkeys and growling dogs and yowling cats and parrots spreading their rainbow wings in an arc on the nose of the plane become shadows and Timothy is sinking into the green murk of the

Land (or Place) of Not, he can still smell the rot of the River Styx, the smell so strong and odious that he weeps.

But now, only his pulse-place held beating between the fingertips of the night nurse, who has Coke-bottle eyeglass lenses and bright-pink skin, lets her know that there is anyone alive in there at all.

The scarlet tear on the crisp white bedsheet quivers.

Timothy thinks, *The Earth was my woman.*

My nubile, healthy, beautiful young woman. He has floated now dreams away from the frothy shit-swirls and rot of the River Styx into long languid pools of green, and into bright velvety colours.

I plunged my hands into the earth the way other men plunge their hands into their women. This thought pleases him. *The Earth Goddess, Rhea.*

Timothy lies in a field of flowers, flowers of glorious crimsons and scarlets and golds, soft mauves, vibrant purples, a teardrop of pink, swollen white flowers, fuchsias and deep blues, deep-purple and velvet pansies, black-eyed Susans with their darkest-night black-eyed centres, pale-white frosted babies' breath. Red-petalled tulips, blood lips raised skyward, sunward. He floats on a carpet of peace, of beauty, and all this he is responsible for.

When he got home from the War he started planting. When he got home from the War he could not stop planting. And now he is right there standing on the acre of land in the middle of the wilds of Scarborough that he got through the VA Land Act. Huge maples and beech trees and elm trees with their magic floating keys surround his acre of land on all four sides. A few poplar trees are placed in between the towering beech and maple trees.

First he dug deep into the earth and poured in cement for a basement, the girls all lined up, roly-poly dolls in diapers and lacy white sunbonnets, on a blanket under the towering green maples beside the glinting white stones on what would become the driveway at the end of which he one day would build the garage. He raised the wooden sides and roof-beams, he hammered in joists, cut out squares of windows, put in insulation, glass panes. He remembers the steely cold taste of nails held in his mouth, a hammer at his hip, and he sawed and hammered and pounded and poured and tarred until, one day, there was Clarice in kelly-green shorts with long shapely golden-tanned legs, white sling-back shoes, on top of the raised high roof, nailing down shingles the colour of burnt-red roses.

His house. His. Built by his own hands from the ground up. Red brick and white clapboard. Now, surveying his proud land, a whole wide acre, his eyes caress each white siding of wood, every red brick. The front door and the storm-porch door and the windowboxes and shutters are painted blue. Three and a half storeys high, and his, all his. The House that Glass built.

In the back of one of the closets in the house there was a secret door hidden by the clothing hanging on the hangers. If you were a troll you could skitter through just fine, but the door was troll-size so that if you were a little girl (and he had little girls) you had to double over, crouch up real tight and small to crawl through, and this small door opened up into a whole other part of the attic, a big, high wide room where sunlight streamed in through a triangle window and dust motes fell through the streaming light like tiny white birds.

But even then he could not stop digging in Rhea. Loving her. He'd built a house on her and now he dug gardens, gardens everywhere. A dozen different kinds of roses and mums and lilies and marigolds and pansies, geraniums, petunias and bleeding hearts, snapdragons, babies' breath, impatiens, rhododendrons, tulips, gladioli, daffodils, violets, crocuses, and more! More! But even this was not enough.

With an endless chain of cigarettes glued to his lips he dug out the earth for fruit trees. Apple, cherry, peach, plum, and pear. And then he planted a chokecherry grove, which bled bright-red berries in autumn, and he laid glittering white stones under the chokecherry grove. Still he could not stop. A grape arbour. Ashes fell into his trouser cuffs, onto the backs of his hands, into his flannel plaid workshirt pocket, onto the ashes of roses carpet in the living room in the house. He looked across his land. And it was not complete.

He is floating further back into his mind and away from the velvet carpet of flowers sitting with Number-Two Daughter, the Dreamer, on the small hillock of land behind the house. The Dreamer, how old? Two? Three? A blaze of fireflies lighted the darkness. He remembers the Dreamer's eyes following the rising and falling of the red tip of his cigarette.

He said to the Dreamer, "How about a raspberry patch? And a strawberry patch too, so Mommy can make us her great pies?" Soft, his voice was. He was weary.

"I guess," the Dreamer sang-said and scuffed the tiny toe of her red sandal into his earth. Never much for words, the Dreamer. And she never actually just spoke words. She either sang them or if not that rhymed them in couplets. He'd never known a child to do that before, but he did not ponder this often. She was, after all, the Dreamer.

"And a whole halo of wild yellow buttercups in the side yard," Timothy said. "With a swing! Two swings! Lilacs by the fence and vines!"

You could read the seasons in his hands. He held them there. He bunched the smoke from burning autumn leaves in his fists and he lassoed winter winds on his fingertips. In spring and summer the pistons and pollen and flower petals painted his hands with their hermaphrodite stains. He thinks of that now, remembers the smell of burning autumn leaves, the pollen staining his fingertips, the dusky, damp rich smell of earth and of the ice rink he made under the hillock every winter where flat land lay and over which he strung tiny midnight-blue lights.

That night. He has never forgotten that night. It makes him feel good, powerful, alive! He and the Dreamer sitting in the darkness on the hot July night, his red cigarette tip rising, falling, and suddenly a whole whirligig cloud of fireflies came out of nowhere, it seemed, dozens and dozens of them whirling and swirling, their tiny white lights like lighted snowflakes, and he remembers thinking, *It is snowing fireflies*. And then, the most uncanny thing, the Dreamer, who rarely spoke, sang-said, *Daddy, tomorrow everything will be covered in firefly snow and safe and hidden again.*

He knew what she meant, all the horrors that had to be hidden in the world, but pretended he didn't, so instead he smiled and started to tell her about the big vegetable garden he planned for that patch of land that lay just beyond them and was as yet untouched by flower or bush or fruit tree. He told her they would have green beans and potatoes, and silky golden corn, radishes and chives, yellow wax beans and cabbages, turnips and cucumbers, beets and carrots, tomatoes big as baseballs! There'd be green onions, and peas, squash, and hundreds of big fat wicked orange pumpkins in the fall for Halloween.

"And more if I can think of it," he said. And then he thought, "An asparagus patch."

And the fireflies came and came, swirling and whirling, snowing their darting white lights.

Tomorrow everything will be covered in firefly snow and safe and hidden again. . . . .

Well, he thinks, floating now lazy as a frog on a log on a hot summer's day, it was done. All of it was done. He remembers the pale-green asparagus looking like skinny ladies dressed up in filmy green finery swaying in summer breezes.

Ah God, but it was good. The fireflies snowing their darting lights and the cicadas singing out their high-wire summer love song from the trees into the hot dark night and the sounds of the birds calling in the ravine that lay just across the narrow road at the foot of their lot and the movement of the raccoons and other creatures who dwelled in that deep, shadowed ravine where a crumbling old mill stood and hundreds of white-and-pale-green trilliums grew among the high reaching-for-the-sky trees, beside a brown brook.

"Daddy," he remembers the Dreamer sang-said, extraordinarily talkative that night (for it was a magic night snowing fireflies, the cicadas singing out hot love at a frenzied pitch). "Daddy, you're taller than God."

And he remembers he laughed a little to disabuse her of that notion, and she sang-said, "Throw a handful of blue stars up into the sky."

He just smiled and pointed to the crescent moon riding the midnight-blue sky, and said, "Look, there's God's eyelash."

"Ahh," the Dreamer breathed in wonderment, and then whispered in song, "You are too taller than God."

God's silver eyelash floating above them.

8.

THE PETRIE DISH. Once when I went to visit Daddy at Sunnydale, I walked into his room as a lady doctor was giving him a rectal examination. A thin white sheet had been drawn around the bed but was left flapping half open. I could see the doctor's gloved finger plunging into his rectum. Daddy lay curled on his side, naked from the waist down, his pale, thin flanks exposed, his knees drawn up, his long-fingered hands clenched into fists under his cheek like a child, and he moaned softly. I backed out of the room, backed out, backed out.

I think my mind went frozen then for a while into something black and cold. Like a black pool of ice, covering me like dark ponds of ice cover fish, protecting them. Protecting me. Later, when I could think at all again and the ice chipped away, I thought, I can understand how I ended up in the petri dish the way I did some time ago, but Daddy too?

In the petri dish, you move round and round at the whim of anyone's hand or instrument, grinning grimly, often gamely, amoebas' tails flicking at your nostrils, and you are helpless even to scratch your nose. Microscopes, probes, needles, pills, endless pills, EEGs, ECGs, needles through bones, spinal taps. All this was a given to me a while ago, but to Daddy?

. . . A long-ago spring afternoon in 1964 and the sun is warm on my cheek though the rays are pale and weak. The sun spans my right cheek and eyelid like long, warm fingers. I sit ensconced in a white wooden lawn chair. It is enough. There is a lap-rug on my knees, a hot-water bottle at my back. They say I am much too thin and must keep warm. They call me hummingbird. And Hemingway, because I sit in the ward hallway, my knees drawn up, a notepad against my knees, writing, always writing. The women patients first said it with scorn, scorn because their minds could not work with such linear logic, follow pale-blue lines, and they'd spit great gobs into my hair. I'd wipe the spit out of my hair and continue writing. Then they would say it with less scorn. Some of the women would even say it with something verging on respect, but at the same time always cursing me when they said it. Saving face.

A huge dark bird – a pterodactyl? – with blue flapping wings hovers by my elbow. Flowers, flowers everywhere lift their pale petals to the pale sun. The grass is damp and green and in places brown and stubby. Foot imprints are in the damp grass. John the Fire-Thrower is trying to fit his feet into the imprints, trying to make his feet fit Others'. Will he become Another? A Brand-New?

Other navy-winged birds, pterodactyls all, float around here and there, lighting, darting, giant keys jingling noisily at their middles. Babble babbles. A steady stream of obscenities. Babble cannot stop his babbling. No one pays attention. *Pay attention*, the teachers always said at my high school, pointers to the blackboard, which all seems a million years ago, light-years away. *Pay attention* when the Keepers walk you down the long, dim underground hallways to the Shock Shop and strap you down so you won't break an arm or leg though people still do break bones. *Pay attention* when they instruct you to open your mouth for the black rubber gag. *Pay attention* when they shove pills in little white paper cups towards you over the double-dutch doors of the nursing station, and *No tonguing them!*

But to Babble no one pays attention. One is probably not supposed to. Even here there is a certain etiquette. Like the gobs of spit. Politeness and mind your manners, please.

For example, no one stares at the soft-skinned-covered holes in the heads of the lobotomies up on B-3 and A-3, one on either side of the skull. Soft and innocent, those two drilled-out bits of skull, as a baby's fontanelle.

Helene, her pale, thin arms weaving like white snakes, dances on a tree trunk, weaving arms, weaving songs, weaving words, worlds. Big Marion from up on B-3, a Violent Ward for Women, flanked by two Keepers, hefts a bright-red, beat-up rubber ball straight into the sun and it spins and spins, spins like it could go on forever, spins higher and higher into the watery-blue sky.

Ahh, breathes Babble, pausing for a moment in his swearing song. Even Helene's ceaselessly weaving arms fold in front of her, motionless, crossed over each other as if in prayer and "Oh-hh," she says, her perfect sun-kissed mouth forming an oval as we all watch the red rubber ball spinning out into space. The boy with the purple burn marks the size of nickels all over his palms stops wringing his hands and grins. Even the few drying-out alcoholics listlessly shuffling brooms around the shuffleboard court pause in their tired game and look skyward, cigarettes dangling from their smeared, painted lips. The red rubber ball spinning. Away. Away. To another planet maybe. A new galaxy. Even the preposterous navy-blue pterodactyls in their winged caps stop jingling the keys at their middles and look.

I blink. And then I remember it is only today. Another day. Everyone goes back to their designated places. Helene's arms weave, the boy with the nickel burn marks wrings his hands. Babble babbles. John the Fire-Thrower has found a good fit for his huge brown shoe. Fats holds up the white pillar on the A-1 porch where he always holds it. That is his job; to hold up the pillar on the porch of A-1 like Sampson. His red beard is wild and tangled and woolly enough for him to be Sampson straining and holding up biblical pillars.

Babble babbles a steady stream of hate.

I lean my cheek hard against the sun and, open-eyed, I see Daddy walking towards my white lawn chair. Daddy, impossibly slender and tall. He is wearing a light-grey spring coat belted at the waist and a hat like the Beaver and Wally's father wears. The hat slants over one blue eye. I can't tell if it's the one with the ragged eyebrow or not because of the slant of

73

the sun and shadows. His tentative smile. Bringing up the rear is Clarice in her robin's-egg-blue skirt and jacket and the little blue hat with a little blue veil, white gloves, white heels, and a white purse held across her arm like a gun. Her smile is strained from point to point and is glass.

Fuckcuntshitdeepwoodsassholeburnshitcocksucker. Babble announces my parents. Daddy's blue eyes shift uneasily and he blushes. He is one of the few grown men I have ever known to blush at swear words. He is embarrassed and searching for something normal, neutral to look at. A flower, perhaps, a squirrel, a stone. Clarice's white-gloved hand flies to her mouth and her blue eyes grow narrow and tiny and hard as blue steel and she stares straight ahead, still with the brittle smile stretched point to point on her face. Someone should have told them not to pay attention. Daddy is beside my lawn chair, Clarice is fast gaining, her teeth glinting like bits of shattered crystal.

The navy-winged pterodactyl beside my chair swoops down on my parents with my monthly report. Daddy squints at it from under the Beaver and Wally's father's hat. My mother says loudly, gathering a smile together, "Is she bathing?"

It is a well-known fact that I am a poor bather since my illness and often dirty rings circle my neck and ring my earlobes.

I gaze straight up into the sky. I wonder whatever became of that red rubber ball.

It was called my nervous breakdown. I was fifteen years old. All that year, Daddy and I would come across one another unexpectedly among the huge leafy-green plants and vibrant-coloured flowers in the garden. Me with my coils of wire and bits of string singing my stories and poems, Daddy sitting on a rock by the rose garden or on the old grey log by the vegetable garden, smoking and staring into space, eyes lost in the stars. We'd look at each other shyly, embarrassed. He taught me to love every living creature, to kill nothing, not even a wasp or snake.

One spring afternoon after a rain he taught me "Inky-Dinky Spider" on the storm porch by the dripping eavestrough and told me that killing a daddy-long-legs was bad luck. He chain-smoked and the ashes fell onto the ashes of roses carpet and into his trouser cuffs.

He saw the desert laid out like a rippling white ocean, like hot shivering snow.

When I was six I caught a flurry of thick grey ashes in my hand as I stood at the edge of the bluffs, thinking they had crossed the great ocean of Europe, and I buried them in the warm white sand on the beach below the bluffs' edge. Although now of course it is known it was only burnt leaves, bits of ashy shrubbery.

9.

I DON'T THINK there is anyone left to confide in about the circumstances of my nervous breakdown. (My mother is dead these nearly seven or eight years, maybe nine. I don't remember.)

It was the blue winter. It was the bluest winter there'd ever been. I would sit in math class looking out the high transom windows, squinting through the spinning dust motes and hazy clouds of pink and white chalk dust, and there below me in the school's parking lot was a winter in blue, all in blue, blue ice spilled across the asphalt, climbed the ugly brick sides of the school.

I became God-infused and I thought that God was unrelenting and cruel and held mysteries deep as the deepest sea. I began to wear nothing but black, black nylons and black blouses and sweaters and black skirts (even black garter belts) and black shoes. I became the Sylvia Plath of the early 1960s. Pale, emaciated, I cupped Export A cigarettes under the curved palm of my hand in the cafeteria and in the girls' washroom in the toilet cubicle and took deep drag after deep drag until I grew dizzy, until I was close to fainting. I drank black coffee.

I took to reading slender volumes of Sylvia Plath, purchased in tiny bookstores and downtown at Britnell's, and read Anne Sexton's poetry in *The New Yorker*. My only friends were Holden Caulfield and Phoebe and Franny, even though she irritated me, and the little boy in the "Kite Day" story. A white rat named Holden that lived in my bedroom in a silver cage was also my friend.

God was infused everywhere in midnight-blue neon, climbing windows, winding through my white hair like frosted blue ribbons. One day the plant on my windowsill was climbing the blue ice on my bedroom window, its wet green leaves flattened like hungry fat lips against the windowpane. I knew then that it could not go on, the blueness, the cold, the God eating me up.

I swallowed a bottle of poison. POISON, written in giant violent-red letters on the side of the bottle, and that spring they sent me away. Black skull and crossbones pictured on the bottle's side. Oh, I knew how terribly wrong things had gone. Clarice had buried me in used Kotex pads the previous summer.

While I was at the sanatorium Daddy sent me funny little notes all written in rhyming couplets. I made him an ashtray out of brown and white mosaic tiles in O.T. I sent him a long apologetic poem about being such a "bad girl" and such a disappointment as his child. I apologize, I apologize, I apologize. One of the student nurses read the poem

77

and said, "I hate to see you so sad, in so much pain. Is this who you really think you are? Bad, shameful, disappointing? I think you are good through and through, decent, and as smart as a whip."

I don't remember the student nurse's name in her blue nurse's training uniform, but I remember her hand lay gentle on my arm as I wept. I remember that she was young, pretty. In institutions you remember every kindness given you and not asked for, begged after.

Clarice sent me scented bits of soap shaped like pink roses and tiny blue penguins and yellow candy kisses.

I thought of getting out, but sometimes it wasn't so bad. There was Naomi with the blue hair, who used to make me cheese and onion sandwiches, and Mary-Anne the Bomb Letter Girl, who had a sweet and kind disposition and was a friend of a sort. There was old Mrs. Phalen, who set fire to the Christmas tree one Christmas, and Clay Clara, who was usually little more demonstrative or pliable than hardened clay, and had gone running with a war whoop in long, lanky giraffe strides down the ward hallway, laughing and shouting at the top of her lungs, "Good for you, Phalen. It's been dull as dishwater around here lately."

I thought of writing my parents and telling them about how some of the women masturbated and defecated in the halls and threw their shitballs around in the Day Room and Dorm, about Clay Clara, who sat on her suitcases Sunday after Sunday saying brightly, "My parents are coming to take me home today." They never did. But in the end I knew it would do no good – maybe with him but not with her. She hated my being grown-up even if grown-up was only fifteen. She made fun of my small breasts and buried me in soiled Kotex one hot late-summer nightmare afternoon. The sky went Dark. I screamed.

And he – he had nothing to do with our sexuality, with any instruction or talk of it, that was left entirely to Clarice. Maybe The Kid is right – it's just those cinders in my brain, nothing but grey ash sifting through my skull that makes me a bit different; nothing but fugues, where I disappear and come back with my fingers laced with tiny razor cuts and my eyes blackened like two bruised grapes.

And anyway I would have done anything to get out of the House that Glass built. And that is exactly what I did. It is called survival and I wanted to survive. And I did get out – didn't I . . . ?

⤺

Timothy has been to the Underworld. He knows this. He dwells in nightmare pools, remembering the Dead where not even the great white blind worms dare travel. Their faces float up to him like balloons, as they did in the Underworld, faces white and doughy from too much starch and too little sunlight, the faces not making sense, drifting by like they did all around him in a slow dance of decay, colourless eyes lost behind eyeglass lenses. He remembers the smeary cream-coloured walls, a leg eaten into, rotted purple like a spoiled grape.

But once, and he does not know if it was a dream but decides it was not, it was all too real a deadening of his own soul when he saw it, he saw Mr. Walton suspended midway up the wall in the alcove by the nursing station in a wheel-chair. His arms were all funny, so uncomfortably posi-tioned, damn man, they seemed likely to break. They were curved around to his back in a white jacket with many strings. It had taken Timothy a moment to realize that poor Mr. Walton had been encased in a strait-jacket. It has been a long while since he has seen one of those, not since . . . not since . . . but he can't remember. The jacket twisting Mr. Walton's arms into Snakes and Ladders.

Helpless.

Mr. Walton's dark eyes behind his eyeglasses were huge and round and as black as a polliwog's, and they rolled wildly about in their sockets like crazed pinballs in a pinball machine.

Timothy had stopped in his shufflings. Held alert for a moment instead of squinting and lost in the usual fog that seemed to emanate from the green walls and the openings of the sliding elevator doors when a new Dead was brought in. He remembered – he remembered, or thought he did, but it was foggy every day there within the stained walls – that only yesterday he had seen Mr. Walton acting quite merry, sitting with a widow lady in a pretty mauve silk dress and flirt-ing outrageously with her while they watched something sliding across the TV screen in the Day Room and smoking one of his smelly lettuce-leaf cigarettes. "No cancer that way. Gu-a-r-a-n-te-ed," he remembered Mr. Walton saying often (incessantly) and thumping his chest and grinning. Only yesterday. Or it had seemed only yesterday. And now today Mr. Walton was hanging lopsided from a wall like a picture no one wants any more, suspended there in a chair, his plump, lumpy body jerking and lurching like a wounded, dying thing.

His feet were odd. They alone were still and tidy. His black street shoes were polished and the black laces carefully laced, and the shoes were neatly, rigidly affixed into metal straps.

The Dead, the Dead. Clever dead, some of them, so as not to appear Dead. There were still the Four Grande Dames. And the Grande Dames' card table. The Four sat with their sticky cups of sweet tea and played canasta. One of them even smoked still, despite the advanced age of eighty-six, carefully dropping her ashes into a grey metal ashtray. She smoked Pall Malls, which a granddaughter in the States sent her two cartons of every month in a pale-blue wrapped box. Grande Dame Number Three would, without fail at some point in the canasta game, let go with an endless stream of urine the colour of a lemon gone rancid from under her many black skirts and crinolines, where it would pool beneath her chair like a stagnant pond. Her black shoes floated in the sewage, her white ankle socks soaked, a purple vein above her ankle pulsing and glistening with the drops of urine until boys came with mops and pails.

Strapped in chairs and fed were the Dead who could not feed themselves and those whose hands could not be trusted not to hit and those who could not be trusted not to fall out of chairs if not strapped in. Those that had to be force-fed always had their mouths hanging open, as if to receive the next pill, or vitamin, the next tablespoon of Maalox, or constipation pill, or the plastic food plunger.

"Hush, don't be like that. Lunch-time, silly boy. Gotta eat and keep up your strength and get healthy, doctor's orders." Dribbles of green and yellowish muck would slide down chins, coil around throats, and dribble down chests.

Timothy floating in his terrible cold sea thinks of Crystabelle again, the one with the fairy-tale name, who once had emerald-green eyes and golden hair and skin the colour of white rose petals. Crystabelle insisted on only one right in the Home and that was to wear the dress she was wed in Mondays to Fridays. Since it was the only thing she'd ever asked for, never so much as a bed pan or an extra blanket on cold nights was begged, this wish was granted. She had been married in the satin gown over seventy years ago. It had been a white floor-length gown but the satin was yellowed now and the lace at the wrists and high neck had also yellowed and was thick with grey filth. What was obviously a floor-length wedding dress had been cut unevenly, in a jagged fashion, and now hung lopsided just below the fairy Crystabelle's knobby blue knees. Crystabelle wore a pair of red Reeboks on her feet and nylon ankle socks neatly folded twice over the tops of her shoes.

Timothy wishes all memory were a slate wiped clean. And he does not know that it is not or if it will be. Knows only dimly that he might have once known things like this.

Timothy himself is sliding into a kind of dizzying euphoria brought on by nightmares. Timothy sees with the lucidness some nightmares bring to the sleeping that, like Aeneas, he has gone down to the Underworld and seen the Dead. But, unlike Aeneas, he has not returned.

10.

TIMOTHY REMEMBERS – or dreams. It is all a dreaming now anyway. He is thinking about marrying Clarice out in Comox, British Columbia. And before that the rain. He was housed the last year of the War in a huge hospital out in Victoria, British Columbia, and he remembers that once it rained for twenty-two days. Or nearly twenty-two. He did not mark off the days with sticks laid in rows or with a piece of chalk on the dim blue walls. But surely it rained for at least twenty-two days. Maybe it was even one hundred days that it rained, and he thought, like Noah gathering up the animals two by two, that Noah or God would reach down their huge hands and gather up the men in the Crazy House in their great arms like so many bunches of flowers and lift them gently into the ark, two by two.

He remembers standing at the wire mesh window and seeing the abundance of green rising up and up like the huge waterlogged plants of Venus. Verdant green. The fog that floated across the lawns of the lost skirted just above the edge of the rich emerald-green grass like the tattered wedding gowns of jilted brides. The Staff wanted him to take a needle, a cup of tea, play cards, have a pill, *sit down*. But he would not. He wound his fingers through the mesh and smelled the damp earth, Rhea, and heard the crying of the rain from the weeping willows that stood like shadowed giants, huge and green and heavy-dripping. The gathered, ragged white skirts of the jilted brides undulated across the lawns and amongst the trees like lost and haunted spirits.

And there was only Timothy, hands wound through the mesh and bars, and the dripping of the trees and Venus.

He remembers he married not long after that day on Venus when all sound was muffled by thick oceans of fog and the steady silver dripping of rainwater. He remembers Clarice wore a little green hat with a green feather in it. Clarice travelled three thousand miles by train across Canada from Toronto to British Columbia to marry him. She travelled all that way and all alone. She was nineteen years old, had buried her father three weeks previously, her father whose bald pate she liked to smother in fluted red kisses when he sat in his armchair reading the funnies. She packed her suit-case by herself because her sisters were jealous of her betrothal and would not help. She had no trousseau. Her brothers thought she was too young to be getting married and would not help.

The housekeeper they'd kept since her mother's death, Jessie, gave her a bone-china teacup and saucer as a wedding gift. It was her only gift.

She sat on the train for all the three thousand miles and drank tea with lemon and two cubes of sugar and read her poetry books with the Latin translations scrawled in the margins. She looked mysterious, a woman travelling alone with a green hat with a green feather in it and little green veil. A world traveller, a woman of intrigue, she was reinventing geography, she was reinventing the entire Earth. The world. When she came for him at the hospital he looked at her blankly. He'd had shock treatments, the doctors told her.

At first he thought she was that new comedienne Lucille Ball, who had appeared in a few movies. She tried to laugh and whipped off her hat, veil, green feather and all, and showed him how her hair was long and chestnut brown and not like Lucy's hair at all. They sat in the Day Room and drank bitter coffee. She told him she had written him every day and sent him socks and scarves and saved tinfoil. She had seen stars placed in the windows of weeping women. Death lists posted. Men with empty eyes moved through the Day Room. One man kept going into a deep crouch and then pitching himself high against the wall trying to fly up it.

Mumblings, rumblings from dead-eyed men.

Timothy told her it had rained for twenty-two days.

He rubbed his eyes. "They say it will come back to me eventually," he said.

"Twenty-two days. Imagine," said Clarice. She thought she was going to cry.

"Saw storms like that in the desert. Of course it was sand not rain. One sandstorm is red and it comes up thick and dense, a solid wall of blood. Saw men buried in it just like it was a red sea."

The blank-eyed men looked out at the dusk darkening into a purple-slashed night.

Clarice went to a hotel room alone that evening and took a bath and drank a gin and tonic and swore she'd make him well.

He chain-smoked and his ashes fell into his slippers and onto the stained yellow linoleum tiles of the Day Room floor. He did not drink more than one sip of his bitter coffee. He was thinking of Clarice, he was thinking of slave girls he'd seen in markets in North Africa with gold rings around their fingers linked by gold chains to their masters' wrists. He'd crashed into the sea three times. He had a big bandage on his head where the bolt from the plane had torn through his skull.

So, thought Clarice, his mind is a little – slippery. She would make him well. Slippery, that was all. Three thousand damn miles and no trousseau and no daddy to give her away like a proper bride were not for nothing!

She'd lived in funny little houses with crooked corners and tilted floors, her daddy one step ahead of the bill collectors all her life and the bread and egg man chased her around the kitchen table with a lascivious smirk on his face. And her mother died when she-was-only-six and now her poor daddy. Dead is dead. She had her little black Confirmation Bible in her purse, but enough was enough. Who was Clarice Magraw if she could not contain and nurture a slippery mind? She had another gin and tonic and smoked a Black Cat cigarette and made plans for the next day.

The next day Clarice in her little green hat with the little green feather went back to the hospital and helped Timothy pack his two duffel bags, and on their way to the church (which she had chosen) she showed him the splendid silver ring he'd put on her ring finger. They were married by two ministers in an Anglican church with two witnesses whom they had dragged off the street. One witness had a wild white cat sitting on his shoulder with one gold eye and one blue eye.

The sky was a pale green on their wedding night and the room was lit by a flickering kerosene lamp where moths danced, and they sat up all night in bed laughing and eating wedding cake and drinking Coca-Cola out of thick green-glass bottles.

That night in bed Timothy tried to whisper something to his bride. "I –" he began.

"Yes, dear."

"I – nothing."

They stayed in the hotel two nights and had tea at the famous Empress Hotel and then they found a little cottage to live in on a beach in Comox.

There is more to remember in this journey through inner cosmos, a possibility of meeting God himself? Timothy scoffs at God, he rails against Him, he wants Him. Timothy remembers the ashes of roses carpet in their house and the big picture window that the starlings and robins flew into thinking it was only air. The blue sky's reflection was caught in the windowpane and the birds flew straight on ahead, trusting the blue, and broke their poor necks. Deceptive, cunning glass. He buried the starlings and robins in the rose garden and among the rhododendrons. He remembered he chain-smoked cigarettes down in two long drags whenever he and the Fly Boys went Up.

He remembers in Quebec he bloodied the face of a man who refused to go and fight in the War. The man had spit in his face, called him a murderer. Timothy remembers he beat and beat at the "zombie's" pinched face until he lay unconscious in the street and Timothy put a sprig of ivy in the "zombie's" buttonhole before going to the nearest bar and ordering a scotch, then another and another, his fingers trembling around the glass under the glossy red sheen of another's blood.

Ah the War, the War, it was everything.

Pack up your troubles in your old kit bag and smile, smile, smile. . . . What's the use of worryin', it never was worthwhile.

He remembers having children, although he cannot recall how many or their names. But those bats, he remembers the bats. They were funny little fellows. Their hands, their fingers were surprisingly human, endearingly so, and when they scuttled across the ground their long fingers travelled ahead of their little rodent faces. Back in Comox above their cottage on the beach were the bat caves.

Clarice is terrified of the bats, but he goes up there every day and sits in the bat caves and draws comfort from their whirring wings, even from their tiny ugly red eyes. He does not even mind the odour of their dung or the insects and maggots that crawl through it. He stays up there with the bats until Clarice rings the dinner bell on the porch calling him to supper. His head hurts. That injury from the War.

"Lucky to be alive," the doctors had said, taking the bolt from his skull and dropping it with a metallic *ping* into an enamel bowl. He gets headaches and sometimes it is hard to think. He remembers a boy dead on Gibraltar. Ian. His best friend. When they liberated the camps, the Jews could not eat the potatoes and bread the Allies had brought them stuffed into their pockets because their stomachs were so shrunken. All used up! The Jews were all used up. The Nazis in the camps tore the still-living fetuses out of their still-living mothers' bellies.

We were all just boys, he thinks, we were all just boys fighting boys in the War. We were all just boys killing boys in the War.

He remembers three times he crashed into the sea. He remembers Christmas-leave in England, fire-bombings. But the War is over now. This knowledge moves through him like a sleepy cry. He feels given up, defeated. He wishes the headaches would stop. The bats climb onto his face and settle over it. The bats' wings cover his entire face. He remembers what he remembers. He goes daily up to the bat caves and listens to their scuttling and hissing sounds, and fact becomes fact. Time is a tunnel and he bids them cover his face and they mount it and spread their wings out across it like huge black autumn leaves.

Strangely human fingers reaching out.

The nurse turns Timothy over onto his other side. "This side all done," she mutters half out loud, half to herself. "Why, there isn't anything to him. His brain has ate him nearly all up." She flicks out the night-light over his bed and, following her white flashlight beam, a single white eye in the darkened room, though a crescent moon thin and golden slides through the sky, she leaves Timothy Glass to his dreaming and the black autumn leaves laid in a shroud across his face in the other dimension of the Land of Not.

～

When The Kid and I got back to Toronto it was autumn and moved swiftly into the winter of my father's agony, and now it is spring again. I like to think he is safer now than he was before at the Home. A sleep deeper than the deepest sleep of natural sleep. Where does he voyage? Another dimension? Where do I voyage in my fugues?

11.

DADDY AND I were walking through a dense snowfall. This was some months back when he was in Sunnydale, the past winter. We were leaving the scene of a crime. A felony. I tell this now to The Kid, who sits drinking Gatorade and playing absentmindedly with one lock of his long dark-auburn curls.

"Why was it a felony?" The Gatorade is orange.

"Well, honey, it sure as hell couldn't be called a misdemeanour! No way! Grampops had a bib around his neck, a big bright-yellow bib."

The Kid's face reddens. "He still ate okay, right?"

"Sure did. Not so much as a crumb dropped from a fork tine."

The television set is on. We do not watch it.

I had gone to visit Daddy in the nursing home and when the elevator doors slid open onto the scent of stale piss and disinfectant I saw my father standing there. Oh, I thought, what has happened to your mouth, all drawn in like fingers pressed tightly together? He was simply standing, a pearl-grey tie at his throat, his hands forever bent in their dog-paws position, his eyes wild and blue. But it was not the mouth, like fingers bunched and drawn and pressed cruelly together, that stopped me up. Stopped me dead in my tracks, made hot-white electricity pour through me, melting me into hot liquid that pooled down into the pointed toes of my high heels. He was wearing a huge bright-yellow bib, out-sized like the stupid cartoon duck Baby Huey wears, the strings tied neatly around his neck.

I was made of electricity, I was pure burning water, nothing human any more. I walked quickly over to him, my smile as glass as Clarice's had ever been, and in one swift movement reached up and untied the bib from around his neck.

"What's that?" he asked, noticing it for the first time.

"Oh it's nothing, Daddy," I said as nonchalant as Gene Kelly dancing in the rain. I am a hot-white wire. I am pure burning, boiling water. I tucked it into my purse. "I'll be back in a minute." He looked in a confused way around him (does the room move, change position from moment to moment?), looking to hills, to white deserts where snow drifts hotter than lava, and I marched to the nursing station where the two boys were dancing with their mops to radio station Rock 102. A nurse was drinking tea from a white Styrofoam cup. I smashed the bib down against the desk. "He does not need this. He *does* not! You *hear* me!"

"It's only like a precautionary thing," the nurse said from under heavily shadowed lids. The boys were dancing up a storm. I did not say another word but walked back towards Daddy, thinking, *Oh, Daddy, I'll get down on my knees now and forgive you for using your arm, the bolt the door the day Clarice hissed over coils of telephone wire to come home.* But I did none of that. Instead I told him to get his coat and golfing cap and gloves and that we would go out for a drink.

"Good-o," he said, hang-dog mouth, begging dog-paws, eyes looking backwards into skull. He once said that opium could do that. Peel your eyes back like two skinned grapes so that you saw into everything.

It takes ten minutes for him to shuffle to his room and back. I help him with his jacket, his arms are Plexiglass run through with wire.

Some things never leave a person, I think as we hit the sidewalk outside of Sunnydale. The gentleman always, he offers me the crook of his elbow to hold on to. A courtly gesture from the little boy who knew how to sit with his mother and aunts and uncles and sip tea in the garden out of fine bone-china cups.

How it snows! In bundles, whole wavering frozen sheets, but we lean into the wind, the snow, his chin tilted at an upwards angle, and we make our way through the streets to a greasy spoon I have taken him to before.

"May – be gone," he says, peering through the snow that blinds us, the streets like archangels' fiery white lashing robes. But no, no there, I see it. Its pale-lit yellow-neon daffodil shivering and flickering faintly through the white robes whirling cruelly around our faces and making our teeth chatter.

The warmth of the Daffodil steams up my glasses and causes Daddy to let out a long whooshing sigh of relief. The owner of the Daffodil, a round rosy-faced Greek man with a bushy black moustache, greets us exuberantly. We have been there many times before. We are barely seated before the Greek proprietor sets two scotches on our table, a little ice, and whips open the menu for Daddy, who, and I guess the Greek proprietor knows this too, can no longer read. Daddy makes a pretence of scanning the menu. Snowflakes melt slowly on his golf cap and disappear.

I suggest a toasted Western and chips. I eat nothing. I am here for serious drinking, for serious forgetting. His speech has grown garbled now, he talks in private anagrams that I can only sometimes decipher. But we drink and the Daffodil is warm — even the pale-green arborite tabletop gives off a warmth, and he loves the Western sandwich and the fat French fries. He eats them with relish. *Not a single crumb falls from a fork tine.* We drink some more, and then some more, and his mouth is not so puckered and drawn in, not like cruel wires or fingers drawn in tight as purse strings. He even smiles and laughs once.

It is twilight when we leave and you cannot see clearly through the swirling snow that the sky has gone blood.

I tell him, "I think about you all the time. All the time."

"All right, all right!" he says, annoyed, and for once in perfect, clear people-English. "Don't beat a dead horse."

We float back to the Home with sun in our bellies, the backs of our throats hot.

Daddy hates going back to Sunnydale and lies down on his bed, his face to the wall. Legs of glass, they could shatter like crystal in my hands and splinter in my fingertips, my palms, leave blood there. His golfing hat still on, pulled a little over his eyes, he begins to sob.

"Come on, Daddy, let's take a spin around the toilets." Which is what I call the pea-green hallways. He doesn't want to go at first but dabs his eyes and blows his nose noisily and we begin our tour of the big square floor that is the Home, his ward, and suddenly and I don't know how but he says we are Russians in the 1917 Russian Revolution, comrades in arms and, arms linked, we stagger and march up and down the green toilets singing loudly, for all we're worth, "'Hey little apple, where are you rolling?'"

He had found a place where he could be a real person again, a bona fide human being, for a little while.

↩

I think of my life and all that I did and can still do and there are so many things he can't do any more and hasn't been able to do for a long time, even at Sunnydale. Even before. I sift through the photographs, curled and yellowed with age at the edges. I do this every evening, searching for clues, searching for truth. I gaze into the shy, laughing face that peeks around the trunk of a big elm tree, an old tire swing dangling from a limb, and in another snap he sits in short pants with bony knees proud to bursting in front of a new hand-carved train set he just got for his seventh birthday. That little boy with the pale-blond hair and funny cowlick

95

(now a silver cowlick there still, still . . .) had no idea it would end this way, so diminished – and, more – gone. It is like a tape recording being erased, but worse – not erased sequentially.

"In the end," the nurses say, "they play with their own shit and tear at their bedsheets with dog teeth."

A clock sitting on a bedside table is now only a lump of plastic that makes annoying ticking-insect sounds, like termites. He was always worried about termites, and at Sunnydale he compulsively checked the drawers of his wardrobe, the door frame, the beams across the walls. Eventually, because Squadron Flight Number 517 was painted on a piece of driftwood, he wrapped it up in plastic and put it in his suitcase and this he hid under his bed.

Sometimes when he stayed at my sister Dinah's house on weekends – as she tried her very best to extend herself in this way to him – he'd wake very early in the morning and be found lying fully clothed downstairs on the couch in the living room with his overnight bag all packed, getting ready to go somewhere as if it were urgent. But no one knew where. Not even Daddy. Backwards maybe? In time? Space?

He had stopped being able to urinate by himself any more and at the Home I had to lower his blue jogging pants and then his underwear and hold his penis in my hand while he peed. I wonder if he ever had a child's curiosity about that odd tubing and if he sometimes examined it in the middle of the night when the nurses would not be passing – the two loose, sliding eggs encased in pinkish skin growing out of a tangled nest of seaweed. Did he sit up suddenly in

96

his bed and yell out like a little kid, "Row! Row! Ho-ho! Ho-ho!" Or did he wonder at the strange pinkish-red tubing patterned with purple vines.

He can't light a fire or chop wood or wear his swell and youthful blue jeans any more. He can't catch fireflies in jars, or polliwogs, or sow seeds and plant flowers, or water and dig and fertilize his beloved garden, or remove tiny green aphids from the beautiful and many varieties of his roses between his fingertips. The radio is a disconnected voice.

Once, at the Home he defecated while lying on the bed when my sister Dinah was there visiting. She cleaned him up and methodically and grimly put fresh underwear and jogging pants on him. She was afraid that if she informed a nurse about the bowel movement and had the nurse clean him up he'd be moved to a worse ward than the one he was on with not even a Crystabelle to hold faded majesty over a ragged court.

He can never kiss a woman again.

And yet he once did these things. He played gin rummy with Clarice in the flickering light of a kerosene lamp. He caught fireflies in jars on hot July nights and brought them to my room, climbing the ashes of roses carpet, and gave them to me to use as night-lights on the condition I let them go before too long. Out my bedroom window they flew in silver. Below the earth on our property there was a root cellar and, among the turnips, the beets and squashes and potatoes and carrots, animals convalesced. Once, we had five baby rabbits whose mother had been killed by a car, all brown flicking antennae-ears and warm soft bodies. I brought him a garter snake with a broken back from the deep ravine behind our house and he splinted the snake's back with popsicle sticks. I called the snake Herman. Herman got better and slid away one late-summer afternoon, smooth and beautiful as a green ribbon winding through grass, making a silky sound. We also had puffy yellow baby chicks, and raccoons with blinded eyes or hurt paws from traps, and birds with broken wings. And there was my white rat named Holden, who lived with me for two years in my bedroom, and who I kept in a metal cage with a metal wheel. Among the musty, pungent smells of damp earth and the clean vegetable smells there was the smell of health becoming.

Monday to Saturday we ate at a yellow Formica table, in a kitchen that was painted egg-yolk yellow and had a sea-green linoleum floor. There were blue windowboxes under the kitchen windows, filled in summer with geraniums and pansies.

On Sundays we ate at a large round oak table in the dining room beside a big oak sideboard, where Clarice kept the pink and blue and white candied roses from her wedding cake. Daddy did the carving with a huge shining knife, cutting perfect slices of meat from roasts and hams. The Sisters Three were shadows hunched over their plates of pork chops or roast beef or candied spareribs. They were vague, foggy lumps in their beds at night. I do not know why that is so, only that it was always so.

One birthday for Dinah and Lillian, Clarice made a circus cake with gumdrops and Smarties for balloons and black-licorice elephants, with linked black-licorice tails, circling the cake, and clowns with red-licorice lips and chocolate-chip eyes and pink-marshmallow faces all dressed up in the funny pants of clowns with outsized chocolate shoes.

Once, Daddy stayed up with me nearly the whole night helping me with a school project. The project was to make a coal mine. We had a cardboard box with the front cut off. We painted it grey inside and outfitted the mine with tiny lights and pulleys made of wire and miniature machinery; shovels fashioned from cardboard and Q-tips, and even shiny blue-black bits of coal from our own coal-burning furnace. I did not win first prize. Nor did I tell him how disappointed I was that I had not. I don't think I mentioned it to him at all. It was like the time I broke my leg when I was five. He said I never made a sound, not so much as a whimper. He never understood that, why I never cried with physical pain, no matter how cruel the pain, or confided emotional pain, no matter how severe. I thought, I can't ask. I never could ask.

Had my parents forgotten that I was tested for mental retardation in Grade One and that they never offered a word of sympathy, or indignation, on my behalf? You don't ask. I never could ask.

My father warned me away from the wild kids, who, on Halloween night, would trample through the garden of an eccentric old woman. She lived in the big white mansion on the hill, which was surrounded by high black iron gates and fences. She was from Russia and my father told me that she missed her country so much that she had made her whole house over here in Canada into a shrine. "She will not get a refrigerator," Daddy would whisper. "And inside her ice-box she keeps little herrings in jars and loaves of black bread."

She did not like Canadians was how he concluded this story. She thought we had no backbone or soul. The only real access we had to her was when the neighbourhood children would feed the three horses that roamed freely in a fenced-off area of her property. And on Halloween, kids dared one another to climb the high black fence and race across her property, even peek in the windows!

Our neighbourhood was as complex as any other, maybe more so with the dusty bluffs, the howling winds in winter, and the steadily lapping grey-blue water below, the bent, gnarled trees and ragged grasses, blazing buttercups and purple wildflowers sprouting up from the grasses, and the deep-shadowed ravines, the mysteries, and God (if one believed) were held in all the little living things. The wildness in Scarborough back then in the early 1950s could inspire a kind of madness, or a feyness, sometimes random cruelties.

There was a drunk who lived in the far end of the neighbourhood in one of the newer houses who beat his wife when he was drunk until one night he fell down the stairs leading to his linoleum-tiled rec room and broke his neck. Rumours flew for months about what the wife might do, where she would go. Would she remarry? Begin dating? Instead, she got a new perm, dyed her hair blonde, applied a brand-new bright-mauve nail polish to her fingernails, and had a swimming pool with an electric-blue cabana beside it put in.

There was the retarded girl, Gay, whom I had befriended and whose arms moved like windmills when she talked, round and round, blowing out her words, urging them on. She wore thick eyeglasses and these were always being stolen from her by the bully boys. I remember frequent trips foraging through the neighbourhood, in the underbrush of the ravine, digging in the sand dunes at the bluffs searching for her glasses for her, her windmill arms whirring crazily, "Oh pl-e-ase, oh oh pl-e-ase, Mag-gie, you *got* to. I ca-can't see nothing."

There were the tough boys who rode motorcycles, Harleys, their heavy black boots gleaming and adorned with chains, colourful scarves bound across their foreheads damp with sweat. They drank rye and rum from the bottle behind the high-school bleachers and in the boys' washrooms.

Three streets over a policeman shot his brains out at breakfast with his police service revolver. His wife found him, blood and eggs and bacon and brains and toast crumbs all swamped together in a gory mixture, his chin resting on the plate edge, his brown eyes wide.

Daddy took us to our cottage every summer and used to let me sit in a mossy cave hidden in a wall of rock that rose up on one side of the cottage and watch the loons gliding across the lake, as if the lake were glass, sliding smoothly and gracefully as ice skaters. At our cottage, I remember lunches on the verandah when my mother placed the teacups on our placemats and said, "These were my mother's who died when I-was-only-six." And we'd all look down at the teacups laid out like tombstones at our places and thank God, thank God, that our mother didn't die when we-were-only-six.

Daddy was a good swimmer and every afternoon it was down to the beach with lawn chairs and floating whale toys and bars of toffee and ice-cold Cokes – the adults had whiskey sours with maraschino cherries – and we'd bake in the sun until we could not stand one more moment of the heat, of sun reddening our bodies like lobsters, and then we'd all dive into the water and swim.

Sometimes I'd swim over to the small cove next to our cottage – perhaps just fifteen, twenty yards away – and bask on the pink rocks, or I'd float among the lily pads, eyeing the big bulging bullfrogs that eyed me back, and watch the tiny mosquitoes and marsh flies float like clouds or hallucinations over the smooth green water. I waved bulrushes around like magic wands, making stories as I waved them, and I twisted wildflowers in my hair and wore water lilies like jewellery in the straps of my bathing suit.

In the tall, reedy water grasses of the cove I was an Indian, or sometimes a great prehistoric snake newly awakened and discovering the world, but most often I was Ophelia in the Shakespeare play I had already read in the attic, with lily pads and seaweed wound through my long flowing white hair. Ophelia dying, dying as golden butterflies danced around my lifeless limbs. Later I'd swim back to the others and we'd bake in the sun again for a little time, eating our melted toffee bars while our parents finished off their warm whiskey sours, the maraschino cherries gone all soft.

We ate dinners of steaks and fried potatoes cooked on a woodstove in the kitchen or roasted chicken and roasted potatoes cooked inside the woodstove oven and stare at the teacups set out at our placemats.

Solemnly.

Nights were flickering kerosene lamps and moths dancing, hypnotized by the flames, drawn, as I would be drawn at fifteen to poison, to the fire, their wings falling dust. Nights were quiet murmuring voices and books read by me and The Sisters Three while Clarice and Daddy drank two or three more whiskey sours and ate peanuts and gumdrops and read their books. Later they played a game of cards (I did not play cards. I hated playing cards). Much later everyone would go to bed.

Blankets and down comforters were piled sky-high and the fire burned low all night, shooting out sparking orange glints in the dark from the great stone fireplace. When I awoke in the mornings I crept past the shadows of The Sisters Three and looked out the window at the mists rising off the lake like white shimmering veils and saw the loons sliding across the glass lake and calling out their eerie alone calls and I'd pinch myself and blink and think, None of this is real. I am not real. None of us are.

We always hated going home from the cottage, packing up our hundreds of books and tins of food and bulgy floating whales and suitcases of clothing and whatever animals we had with us, but once in the car driving down dusty country roads our moods would lift and Clarice always sang lustily, loudly, every single year without fail or missing a beat, "There's food around the corner, there's food around the corner, oh thank Christ, there's food around the corner!" as we reached the tiny motel-restaurant at the midway point home.

Once we were back in the white-gravel drive shaded by the green maple trees that cast their giant shadows over the hood of the car, when the car was unpacked, Daddy would light a cigarette and squint into the smoke and say, "Sorry to be home?"

"Oh school and all – all that," I'd answer, digging my toes into the glinting gravel.

"Dreamer, dreamer." And he'd shake his head and grind his cigarette out beneath the heel of his shoe. I was left to ponder if being home was any more real than the fairyland we'd just left behind, the magic lagoon of our cottage where I was a prehistoric reptile discovering the brand-new world for the first time, or a forever dying and beautiful Ophelia, flowers and seaweed wound through my hair.

~

Timothy sits in the flickering light of the kerosene lamps, the moths beating their dusky wings against the cottage screens. He cocks his head, listening to their magical beat, and smiles.

12.

ONCE, TIMOTHY HEARD a girl falling, falling down from the sky. He is hearing her again. The first time he heard the girl fall to the Earth from the sky was in the desert. They had just come back from a night mission, crept back at dawn, searchlights ready to grab you and seize you and hurl you down from the sky. The Fly Boys had all been exhausted and, as was their habit on returning from missions like this, they smoked opium and languidly petted their monkeys and ragged dogs and wild cats. The parrots shone in night rainbows in the oncoming dawn and in the lights of the small fires where the Fly Boys were making billies of tea.

That was the first time he had the opium dream of the falling girl.

Of hearing her.

Fall.

Like the wind.

He does not have the opium dream of the falling girl again until he has reached the destination of the Place of Not. Where many things are possible. He dreams it as he dreamed it then. The opium has seared back his eyeballs, peeled them like two bloody grapes deep into his skull and left his eyeholes torn and wide open. He does not see her. But he hears her and he knows it is a girl falling from the sky. Opium dreams do that. They know what they know. She falls and falls. He knows, though he cannot see her, that she is wearing a blue silk dress and it flaps around her like silk wings as she makes her night-fall.

At first he hears only a rush, and thinks, That is the wind. But as the wind rushes on and on in the longest of falls it begins to sing and whistle and he knows it is a girl in a blue silk dress falling from the sky and sounding like the wind singing in her deathly rush. He knows too after a while that she is an angel cast out of Heaven to Earth to die again. He listens in vain to the sorrowful sighing, the terrible oncoming rush of wind. His heart pounds. He thinks perhaps he has fallen in love with the girl he is hearing falling from the sky. His heart begins to pound harder. Her hair, he suddenly knows, is streaming out behind her like fire and curling in her wind, in her long fall.

He has crashed three times into the sea. He has seen men die. Wounded. Earth blackened. He will stand up and run around and around the desert in the cold purple dawn with his arms outstretched and catch the beautiful girl in the blue silk dress that flaps around her ankles like silken wings, run around and around for hours (how long does it take to fall from sky to Earth?) and capture her up in his two good arms like she has always been meant to fall into them. Then they will escape from this damn War, find an oasis in the desert where there is no War, only birds bright as orange and yellow fire run through with the lush green of limes and a midnight-blue pool of the coldest water, and fat figs and plums hanging from shading trees, tiny pink flowers growing out of rocks.

They will live there until the War is over and he will stroke her blue silk wings wrapped around her slender white ankles, a bird tucking in its wings for sleep. Then they will move to England and find a small cottage and have children, a family, a garden, do weekly shopping. Ah, it is a wonderful dream, a wonderful plan, and he runs and runs around the desert, his heart pounding and singing, and he hears the onrushing, the sighing of her heart. He calls, "I will save you! I will catch you! I have two good arms here just for you! Just for you!" His heart is an anvil, a motor pounding in a machine.

But that is all. Only the sound of her wind onrushing. She never falls to the Earth much less into his arms. And yet he knew, he *knew* it was an angel in a blue silk dress cast down from Heaven to Earth to die again, falling to Earth, making the sound of the wind, her hair streaming out behind her like fire.

But only the sound of wind, of her falling, only that.

The opium dream ends differently in the Land of Not. He hears her onrushing. He knows her blue silk dress flaps around her ankles like silk wings and then, his heart lurching, he hears a sickening *thack-splat* sound. A splattering of the one who has finally fallen after all these years to Earth and met it full on, arms outstretched as if nailed on a cross, her beautiful blue silk dress all blood, her silken wings broken, the stream of fire that was her hair curling into dying grey embers.

When the nurse checks on Timothy Glass in the night she whispers, surprised, "Why, there's a tear on his cheek." But then she thinks it is only an involuntary reaction, too much mucus in the eyes probably, nothing to actually do with *feeling*, not real feelings, after all, he's in a coma. She takes a tissue from the neat blue and white cardboard box on the bedside table and wipes the tear from Timothy Glass's cheek. She crumples the tissue in her hand and on her way out of the room throws it in the wastebasket.

Timothy crashes into the sea. Oh it is awful, it is awful. The mascots, the dogs and the birds, the monkeys and yowling cats and parrots in the colours of long glasses of lemonade and suns at dusk and twilight are all in the sea too. Three Fly Boys have to hold one man up while they tread water. The man's back is broken. There are some Mae Wests that have not been burned with the burning plane. Timothy clutches Reginald, his pet monkey, who rides his neck and chatters and screams in terror. Dogs drown as the hours tick by, their ever-trusting eyes linked to their masters'. The sea grows black. The sky grows dark. And cold. Reginald sobs monkey tears and clings to Timothy. It is so dark now that the sea is slick black, like oil, like dense crushed black velvet, something suffocating. The Fly Boys cannot see one another any longer in the dark. They have lost six cats, three dogs, one parrot, two monkeys; the creatures' yellow and orange and green and brown eyes filled with a silent shriek of terror as they sink beneath the black water.

The Fly Boys sing to keep up their courage. They do not know if they will be picked up and they do not know if they are picked up if it will be one of their own ships or one of the enemies'. One Fly Boy weeps into his orange cat's fur, the cat perched parrotlike on his shoulder, shivering and shaking and making soft, pitiful cries.

The Fly Boys sing. They sing, *We are poor little lambs who have lost our way, baa, baa, baa. . . .* The words sound eerie and alone, like whispered howls in the dark. Their words join them, these floating separate islands of Fly Boys, blinded by dark, like prayers.

At last (and who knew hours any more after a time of the dogs and men drowning and the monkeys weeping and parrots screaming and the cats stopped-up with terror) one of the Allied ships picks them up. Once Timothy is aboard, Reginald hunkered under his arm, and has a blanket over him and his ration of rum, he sits and smooths Reginald's wet fur and dries it. Coos to him. Calls him "buddy" and "good little guy." "You still got your bandanna, Reg, old bud," he tells the little monkey. Reginald is very proud and possessive of a red bandanna that he always wears around his neck on every trip Up. Once Reginald is calmed a little and has a bit of bread to eat and some chocolate from one of the seamen's chocolate rations, Timothy goes to the rail of the ship and looks out into the black sea where he had spent so many hours, where cats and dogs, parrots and monkeys and men he had cared for, loved, yes loved, were no more, and buried deep, deep. . . .

He thinks he might be able to read something in this cold dark-black sea, some clue as to why what happened happened. He looks and looks at the sea and in the end it tells him nothing.

It is smooth and flat as a plate of glass.

Timothy Glass is looking for God.

Baa, baa, baa . . .

13.

WHEN I WOKE up a few minutes ago, the auras were shooting red and silver stars, an emerald-green comet tail streaked my eyelids. My eyes ache and my head aches in both temples. I can feel those blue lines beating like a drummer's sticks. One of those. I think of Beth-Ann's football helmet stashed in the upper shelf of my closet. Photographs with various small notes written on the backs of them that I was going through late into the night litter my entire bed like messages fallen from the night sky onto my blankets. Automatically I reach over to my bedside table, the drawer, and take out a bottle of large orange capsules. Valproic Acid. My particular antidote for the poison that poisons me. The capsules are stuck against the side of the huge plastic drugstore bottle like fat orange bugs. Ominous. I take two by chewing, without water. They taste foul. Maybe a football helmet would be a better solution. My hands are sweating. My head feels empty and full at the same time. This is not good.

I can hear The Kid singing in the shower. A few minutes later he comes whistling down the hall to my room, a towel wrapped around his waist. His long hair, which falls to his shoulders and flies out behind him like a splendid dark-golden robe when he runs or rides his bike, grows curlier with water and steam rather than straighter.

The Kid stops whistling. Standing in the doorway of my room. Me in my bed with my photographs, rubbing my temples.

"Boy, Mom, your eyes are bugging out of your head."

"Gorgeous as always, no?"

"I'm going to phone an ambulance. You're going to have a seizure. Have you taken your pills?" Already he is moving towards the telephone totally in command, all business. He has been doing this since he was six years old.

"No. Don't. Please. It'll happen and it'll be bad and it'll be over and that's all." Pleading, "Besides, I took the Acid."

He turns. I see the wounded look in his eyes. Dark as two black opals, those eyes, set in that marvellously pale translucent skin to bear witness. Yet again. My beautiful kid. God-touched. Even without a father. Afraid to bear witness even after numerous times — fifty, sixty times? — at the age of four and five and six. Phoning ambulances, even then; 911 was his area code. What have I done to him? The Kid?

My own kid?

The Kid.

"I'm going to phone the ambulance anyway. Bringing you tea or even a shot of scotch doesn't make the mixed-upness or badness and empty things go away," he says. Already he is dialling the hospital for an ambulance.

My nightgown is soaked through with sweat. My hands grip the bedsheets. A photograph curls damp and wrinkled under my hand. The auras are fiery explosions under my eyelids. I hear him give the address and say, "My mom is an epileptic. She's going to hit any minute." Then without another word he turns and leaves my room to go to his room down the hall to get dressed as fast as he can so he can be with me when it hits and wait until the ambulance arrives.

Just The Kid sitting by me alone when it hit and then the ambulance arrived. Later, after I've been to the Emergency at the hospital and had the IV filled with Valproic Acid and my blood levels read, I come home again and crumple on the bed among the photographs.

"I don't understand. The auras are getting worse and worse."

The Kid sits down on the edge of my bed and puts his hand over mine, which is outstretched on a pile of photographs of Fly Boys in training. Parachutes spread out like giant moth wings across the hard brown ground. Or they are alien pods.

"Maybe this is too much for you, Mom. I mean trying to figure out Grampops and all that and the whole Glass Family before Grampops dies. And I mean I know you don't want him to die but, Mom, he's going to. He's in a *coma*."

I say in a muffled voice, "It's what happened all those years ago. Why he did what he did."

The Kid grows silent. For years he said he remembered nothing of that Night of the Knife, of Shadow. (Later, when he was older, ten or eleven, I told him about it and he said he didn't remember anything.) But this year in his Grade Twelve English class, the students were given an assignment to write ten poems. The Kid wrote ten very good poems. One of the poems was called "The Intruder." It was about that night and says things in it that I never told him. When I did tell him about it I said simply, angrily – angry at Daddy – "I was raped in my bed when you were four years old and you were sleeping in the bed beside me and I phoned Grampops for help and do you know what he said! Do you know what he said! He said, "Well, what do you expect me to do about it?" The Kid said he did not want to think about it. We never spoke of it again. And then this poem, "The Intruder," suddenly appeared with details, I mean details, that he could not have known. "The Intruder stopped up her mouth, it was Darker than dark night. . . ."

He got an A+ on his assignment.

"Who knows," he finally says, simply. "Grampops is Grampops."

There is truth in that. "Maybe I will take it a little easier on the writing and the photographs and stuff, honey," I say, mainly to mollify him.

"You okay to be alone?" he asks.

"Yeah, sure. In fact, I was thinking of going out for a walk, just around the neighbourhood. It's a beautiful spring day and the air might clear my head. Don't worry, they gave me that IV."

"Take your pills with you."

"I will. What are you doing today?"

"Going riding downtown with the Boys."

Ah, the ten Chinese boys and one dark-stained, walnut-skinned Pakistani boy with my pale moon with dark star eyes racing among them like an oracle.

"Okay, I'll see you at supper then."

The Kid and I part at the house gate. I watch him ride off. It is Saturday, a beautiful Saturday in early spring and surprisingly warm. I put on blue jeans and a sweater, a pair of boots with fur around the tops, and take a pair of gloves and my purse filled with the necessities – cigarettes, lighters, bottles of pills, notepaper and pens, a lipstick and a blush-on case with a small mirror, money, some photographs, and a bit of paper I'd found the night before with faded handwriting and some sort of sketch on it.

I light a cigarette and shove one hand in my pocket and begin walking south towards Gerrard Street, my purse swinging on my shoulder. I bring the cigarette smoke deep into my lungs, where it coils thick and feels good. My white hair flies back in the wind. The sky is an ochre-blue.

I walk along Gerrard listening to the whisper of saris, passing doughnut shops and dingy bars, and thinking about epilepsy. There is something magical about epilepsy, some magic to cause that short, that sparking in the brain. Daddy never understood that, the magic lining beneath the illness.

He did not know how to greet me when I returned from the Country of Fugue – more than that, he seldom ever knew when I was entering that strange and eerie geography, that other realm where I imagine language is garbled and sleep only a dream rumoured of.

He had never woken me from my nightmares, which were frequent and loud when I lived at home. The next morning he'd comment, "Boy, you were having one bang-up humdinger of a nightmare last night." When I asked him why he did not wake me he'd adjust his pipe in his mouth, or fiddle with a shirt button, or light the hundredth cigarette of the day and shrug, his eyes vague and disinterested.

Or, I would find myself suddenly "coming to" in the car with Daddy bent low behind the wheel, burning rubber, my nose pressed at an awkward angle against the window, sitting beside my father, my mother, her mouth grim, her purse held in front of her like a battleshield as they raced me to yet another hospital because of another seizure on nights that The Kid and I slept over. My brain would be filled up dangerously and sparking and emptying at the same time at a terrifying speed like a river being drained, auras sparking, dancing, eyes bulging so far out of their sockets that I felt they were going to pop out altogether. One doctor said to me at one hospital, "Your eyes are protruding like crazy." And promptly disappeared from the examining room.

At other times, oddly, he would react to a fit without even so much as a comment or a raised eyebrow. One such occasion was after I had a seizure in his car, the first of my seizures he'd ever witnessed. When it was over, after he'd pulled over to the side of the road and taken the cigarette from my hand and was assured it was all over and done with, he drove me in my shell-shocked state over to his house, where we ate a lunch of soft-boiled eggs and tiny triangles of buttered toast and then he drove me home to the slum without a word about the seizure.

Once, he drove me to a hospital Emergency and the doctor who had seen me, a doctor with a frizzy dark beard and thin, long brown hands said, "She had the jerking fit because she has a cold and is coughing." Clarice made a face like she could spit, but Daddy said only later in a mild voice that he thought the doctor's diagnosis inadequate. "Because during it you rose five feet off the floor like a bird taking wing."

I was an epileptic. It was staring them more than rather dramatically in the face and yet they made no real attempt to define it or accept it for what it was. Epilepsy. That awful word. It was just the Dreamer dreaming crazy. It was not until three years later, after my parents had borne witness to many fits, that a good, kind doctor, whom I call Friend and All Mine, treated me for exhaustion and shattered nerves in hospital and became immediately suspicious of the blanks in my eyes. He set up tests for epilepsy, an EEG, and I was put on the Valproic Acid then, a medication for epilepsy, although not as commonly known as Dilantin. This Famous-Friend Doctor, who is kind and all mine, is still my shrink. The Kid, who had been a witness to these seizures since he was four years old and terrified, and often thought back then that I was dying, was, even though tearful and weeping, more helpful and responsible than Daddy or Clarice ever were.

The Country of Fugue – where people exist, walk around, say things but know nothing of their presence in that country or what language they speak or that they speak at all, are unaware they are inhabitants at the time of such a place – was beyond Daddy. The Kid knew. He understood the magic inherent in the thing. Once, on half returning from that Country of Fugue, I suddenly found The Kid's small hand wrapped around mine, pulling me rapidly, rather frantically out of a smoke shop, and I heard a steady stream of curse words coming from a mouth (mine?) aimed at the startled Vietnamese proprietor, then The Kid saying, "Come on, Mom, you're at that Other Place."

Another time on just returning from the Country of Fugue, passport stamped, I found my eyes (mine again) looking at The Kid across the coffee table. He blinked and said, "You're back."

God, he's a good kid.

Suddenly my head aches just from all these thoughts, thinking of the peculiar zeros in my father's and my mother's way of going along with the seizures, as if it were normal when they must have known it was not. I find a really down-and-out bar along Gerrard Street with an Irish name and filthy windows beside a take-out chicken joint and go in there. There, this is what I want, something as down and out as my brain, as my shrivelled soul. Inside, it is mercifully gloomy and the beer is cold. I tilt the bottle back and drink half of it in two swallows. I sit back and light a cigarette and rummage through my purse for the photographs and the folded bit of paper I'd found in the albums last night.

I spread the photographs and square of paper soft as dust out around me on the wooden table, which is pocked with cigarette burns. I drain the beer. It is good and cold. I order another. A photograph of my father when he was five or six lying, eyes closed, in a huge pile of autumn leaves, white sunlight streaming down on him; the expression on his face is one of pure bliss. I study it and study it. So normal. Happy. Were the seeds of Alzheimer's lurking there then?

Were the mysterious blanks, the blocks, that appeared in his actions throughout his life and mine already opening doors in his head?

Or were these caused by the War?

Another photograph of the base where he trained. The bleak brown barracks sit unremittingly side by side, row after row. The ground is flat, without trees or a single bush, hard, unforgiving. It appears deserted of human habitation, a hard sun shines down cold white, the parachutes lie unfurled like the wings of great dead moths or sinister pods set out in this desolate place by an evil other-worldly race. Scrawled on the back of this is *Home. Moonrock.* You can imagine that there is no wind, never even the slightest breeze in this Moonrock home of his for however long his training was, six months, I think, before going overseas.

I turn up another small black-and-white snap and know it immediately. When we were children he would show us this picture. It was of his horse at the farm he worked on in summers from the time he was five until he was eighteen. A horse with a low-slung back and flicking tail, huge mottled hooves, alert ears. Scrawled on the back of this, *Old Bob.*

In another photograph: Ian Glass. He had the same last name as my father. Ian Glass stands beside my father. Their arms are draped easily around each other's waists. They are smiling broadly, standing in front of the plane. Ian Glass is also fair-haired and I imagine blue-eyed. Young. Nineteen. Twenty. Looks a lot like my father, the noble chin and the clear, steady eyes. On the back of this is written *Ian and Lady and me.* "Lady" would be the plane. As I drink my beer, my mind seems more focused than dulled on the cold brew. I am trying to place pieces together slowly, slowly, intricate parts of a puzzle that may one day answer, *Well, what do you expect me to do about it?* Answer the truth that is the Glasses. I suck down cigarette smoke.

I order another beer, and turn over another snapshot. Several grizzled-faced, poorly dressed men are having a heated argument a few tables down. A beer bottle crashes, shattering, a chair topples. I don't care. I'm concentrating. Besides I've been here before and no one ever gets kicked out of this place.

The next snapshot makes me shiver a little, as if the air-conditioning has suddenly been turned on. It is a photograph of the Rock of Gibraltar. Nothing more. No people standing there. It looks very white and jagged. On the back of this he has written only *Ian Glass / 42*. The year of Ian's death on Gibraltar. *Best damn friend in the whole damn War, best damn friend in the whole damn world*, Daddy used to say.

Clarice confided once, "Daddy said if we ever had a boy baby we'd have named him Ian. But of course we had only girls."

There is a photograph of Clarice in a swimsuit holding a speckled trout up on a fish line, sparkles of water flash off the dead trout. Clarice's hair is shorter, pinned up maybe, and curlier. She is perhaps seventeen years old. On the back of this he has written *Up at the Lake with my Sweetheart and big trout, 1938*.

One more beer and then home. And one more bit of memorabilia to look at. This is not a photograph, not one of those tiny two-by-four black-and-white snaps with dates and names scrawled on the back, but a soft, soft square of white paper with a drawing on it obviously made by my father, whose drawings I know well as he used to leave little caricatures of people he knew or politicians, writers, famous singers and actors all around the house. This is a curious drawing, unlike his others. Not a caricature or a cartoon. It is done in coloured inks, the inks faded and smeared, but I can make out the figure of a woman in a softly folding blue dress with fiery-orange hair falling down through a cloud. Underneath the drawing he has written a name. "Isadora Wind."

Suddenly I want to leave. What magic did my father know after all? What bewitchment was held in his opium dreams? I know little of opium, cause and effect, only that coming off it is very hard. I gather up the photographs, Old Bob, Gibraltar gleaming cold-white and alone, parachutes like broken moth wings, evil pods, cold, bleak barracks, dead, smiling boys, Clarice before she bought her breasts. A little boy lying in a pile of autumn leaves, an expression of pure bliss on his face.

I stuff them all into my purse along with my cigarettes and walk out into the sunshine. I remember Daddy at the Home turning to me on one of my last visits, looking straight at me and saying, "You know, I don't have the slightest idea who you are."

Walking home along Gerrard Street I am suddenly weeping, hard, racking sobs like a small child cries, inconsolable with grieving for a lost parent or for a beloved creature. I see that Daddy at last understood the devious magic beneath the lining of the illness, for part of him must have known in that moment when he no longer knew who I was but saw me and sensed I knew him, that he had entered another place, mysterious and lawless and as distant from the rest of the world as the farthest star, and that that was where he had to exist.

Alone.

Utterly.

Utterly.

14.

GOD, I'M TIRED. Just want to sleep, Timothy thinks.
Remembering so much, seeing so much, the girls, Dreamer
with her white hair, humming her stories, Princess – Rachel
– with her red nail polish and wonderful figure, him old
enough to have a wife die on him, cooling against his skin
like cold clay. Yet it seems only a moment ago there was
Clarice in her little green hat with the little green feather
and veil and they were married and sitting in a brass bed in
a hotel eating wedding cake and laughing, moths dropping
their dusky wings around the kerosene lamps. And Dinah
and Lillian eating a circus birthday cake and biting their silly
stuffed monkeys' ears, and Father and him going to the
Home for Crippled and Retarded Children. Was he five?
No, for the Children vanish, and he's stopped right up; can't
be five, must be eighteen.

He never thought he'd see the desolate hunk of moon-
scape again and alone. What he and the other Fly Boys

called Moonrock was the Basic Training Camp where the brown barracks stood, hundreds of them, the colour of mud. They were set up on land as hard and flat and ungiving as stone. It was like living on the far side of the moon, Timothy used to say, where you never expected to see light or the friendly moon face.

Some may be buried there too under Moonrock, Timothy thinks now, hunched over by the great white blind sleeping worms. He is listening to their breathing, steady in-out. If he can hear breath he's not quite yet dead. And yet he can see the whole bleak place of Moonrock. Their flight instructor was called Crazy Bulldog. Crazy because he was, Bulldog because he had sharp, pointed teeth and a mouth like a bulldog, jowls shaking when he roared at the Fly Boys, which was frequently. He kept a loaded gun on his desk in the class on flight instruction. He said anyone who talked or whispered out of turn in his class would be shot.

Christ, Timothy thinks, sitting now in the classroom, nineteen and barely shaving, Bulldog. He doesn't care that they're just boys from small towns out West or from funny little pink and blue houses Down East or, like him, from bigger cities like Toronto and Vancouver or, like Max Luc, from Hull, Quebec. The green murk has receded, the great white worms have disappeared into their own blind eyes, and there is nothing but Moonrock and the floating chalk dust and Crazy Bulldog and his gun propped up on his desk against a book for better firing leverage.

Yes, Timothy thinks, sitting ramrod straight in class, even his eyebrows and mouth gone into rigid lines, there are rumours he's buried a few under Moonrock's ungiving barracks, the cold Moonrock ground. I'm no coward. There was that gang I took on at Danforth and the boy who stole my eyebrow in my first fist fight and I never even winced, and a fight with a cousin and that crazy damn draughtsman teacher we had in Grade Ten at Danforth Tech who used to slug you across the head with a two-by-four till your brains rang like a tuning fork. Just then the sharp whistle of a bullet sparked and cracked loud in the air and the airmen's heads all turned and there was Max Luc, the kid from Hull, with the tip of his ear blown away in a wash of blood. The room grew still.

Listen up, ya morons.

Max Luc cried out but no one made a sound, not even a muttered "Jesus" beneath breath because they could be next. The tip of Max Luc's ear lay on the desktop like a bloody pearl earring.

Crazy Bulldog continued the class on flight instruction and Max Luc bled, whimpering softly. Timothy thought how much he would have liked to have hit his draughtsman teacher just one time hard with a two-by-four so that his blasted brains would ring like a goddamn tuning fork! The tip of Max Luc's ear lay on the desk until the end of the class like a shimmering red dewdrop.

At chow-time they whispered, "He's buried some under Moonrock. Under this godforsaken ground." But who knows what is rumour, what is truth?

No joke either maybe about bodies being buried. Anyone could disappear here, on Moonrock. Not only that, there was the whole ordeal of getting into the army in the first place. There wasn't an orifice of your body they didn't probe, balls and cock and ass too, and there was no amount of teeth the army doctors wouldn't hesitate to pull in one sitting if they deemed it necessary. (Air pressure in the plane's cabin could cause some men's teeth and jaws awful pain and so it was often necessary to pull many teeth, sometimes all of them.) They jabbed you full of needles, and by the time you got to Moonrock you'd been scoured inside out in a room filled with hundreds of naked men and half of you was damn near gone anyway.

So when you stepped off the train onto bleak Moonrock with the wind howling through the treeless land around the shit-coloured barracks, you could just about see yourself disappearing in a godforsaken place like that forever.

Moonrock held its secrets and, dead bodies or no, everyone disappeared a little one way or another.

Crazy Bulldog was crazy all right. When he took them Up the first time for practical flight training – hollering at the Fly Boys to sing "Off we go into the wild blue yonder" (*and loud with guts, ya morons!*) "climbing high into the sun" – he announced that he had never gotten the mechanics of landing a plane right so he simply closed his eyes and prayed and left the landing of the plane in the lap of God.

Timothy Glass remembers saying to his Number-Two Daughter, Maggie, "I think I'm losing my mind." Then putting his head in his hands.

This was at Sunnydale. One of the nurses was instructing Maggie to tell the cab driver that would be picking Maggie and Timothy up to take him to an eye doctor's appointment, "Oh, just tell the driver you've got an old man with you." The nurse fluttered her hands out and smiled. Timothy looked up then, his eyes hollowed out and peeled back and bloody, his mouth turned down in a bitter, ruined line, the pain in his voice unbearable to Maggie. "I hate being an Old Man," he said.

Said just that, plain and simple.

His head bent.

And that was all.

It was enough.

Timothy is thinking, full of joy, I had children. Girls, and I remember some of them! What closet, what space, what deep grotto with these rich secrets in the Place of Not has he finally managed to slide into? His children, all girls. There were three, no four. One was Princess. He remembers this because the family was going to the cottage, he and Clarice — and for this instant he remembers Clarice was his wife who died, just up and died in bed beside him one night, her skin cooling in his arms. He remembers when he awoke in the morning he could not wake her, and then his fingers went to her pulse-place and when there was no answering beat he buried his head against her neck, and wept.

But no, they are going to their summer cottage all of them. All the Glass girls. Clarice, young and leggy with long curly chestnut-brown hair and small breasts. Her breasts before the implants were high and delicate, and tiny as a china figurine's. He never saw why she had to buy those big deals like flour sacks anyway. He thinks they were singing, "It's a long way to Tipperary, it's a long way to go," or some such War song because they always did. He'd taught them all the songs, from "Praise the Lord and Pass the Ammunition" to "We Are Poor Little Lambs" to "The Wild Blue Yonder," and he joked about their mother being the quartermaster as she served up their nightly suppers.

He remembered his small children as they marched around the kitchen with brooms and dust mops gaily singing War songs. But, yes, a happy trip to their summer cottage, tufts of hair from the big collie rising in the back seat of the car in thick smoky-blue clouds, Princess manicuring her nails and bitching bitterly about the damn dog hairs sticking to her nail polish and to her bottle-blonde, hair-sprayed bouffant. And the twins, ah names, names, he remembers their names. Lillian and Dinah playing with their stuffed monkeys in the back seat and biting the stuffed monkeys' rubber ears. Once, when one of the monkeys flew out of the car window, he remembers he had to back up for it as Lillian howled, "MONKEY!"

Clouds of fishflies and mosquitoes rose over the marshes and bogs like shimmering hallucinations. Wild brown brambles and swamp bushes, tall, stark, blackened trees, faded water lilies, limp in the heat, Queen Anne's lace and yellow wildflowers growing along the side of the road by the pink and white walls of rock that rose up along either side.

There was the occasional croak of a big bullfrog looking for his supper, his long thin red tongue coiling out for flies. The other daughter – that one – Maggie, Number Two, the Dreamer, she was just sitting there humming stories to herself. She bothered him. He often thought that, of all his children, she was most like him. They were singing and they had a picnic lunch and Clarice had her bare feet up, long beautiful tanned legs raised up and bent so that the flats of her bare feet were firm against the dashboard and his brood was safe and happy. Sun shining, blue, blue sky, little white tufts of clouds, tiny pale-yellow butterflies the colour of butter. A perfect closet to have cleverly slid into.

But what is this! A huge rumbling, and a thick stream of purple exhaust on the wrong side of the road thundering straight down towards them in the form of a two-ton truck and there's nowhere to go, nowhere to pass, not even a ditch to crash into, and he hears the Dreamer's voice small, almost imperceptible, *"Daddy . . ."*

It was a nightmare of a moment — minutes? It seemed forever, the two-tonner passed so close by them that all the paint was peeled off one side of Timothy's station wagon. When the truck had passed he stopped the car at the edge of the road and sat there shaking for a full ten minutes. Dinah and Lillian were crying. Clarice cursed softly, her hands trembling. Princess moaned and wept and swore in sighs. The Dreamer sat and hummed and rocked. But he had saved them, saved them; they could have all been killed in a minute flat.

The happy singing is gone, and the bright-blue sky, and the little yellow butterflies the colour of butter, and there is only this: Timothy Glass deep in a grotto of a Place of Not and what good had it done anyhow? Where are his brood now? His girls? Clarice is dead. His daughters? Three? Four? Where are they now? Were they pretty? Did they marry? How old is he? Is he three? Five? Old? Did he have four daughters? Five? More? The blind worms sleep coiled in their cold white reptilian skins.

Mother?

Sister Kate?

May I sit down here in the kitchen with you and have a cup of cocoa before I have to go up to bed?

15.

I WAS NEVER once allowed to mention the sanatorium to my family when I returned home from it, though I'd spent quite a long while there. It was as if two years of my life had vanished, had never been. Naomi with her blue hair and cheese and onion sandwiches, Helene dancing on tree trunks, weaving spells of magic in the first pale light of morning, Babble babbling, the boy with the nickel-size burns on the palms of his hands and a purple scar the length and shape of a sabre on his back, or Clay Clara, Sunday after Sunday sitting on her suitcases and saying, "My parents are coming to take me home today," with such brightness in her voice.

Vanished, all of them. Ghosts gagged and bound and drifting through my skull.

But once Clarice surprised me. I was seventeen years old and had been home from the sanatorium for a few months and I was sitting at the kitchen table after school drinking a

Coke. Suddenly Clarice came into the kitchen and slid down into her chair at the head of the table, puffing on a cigarette, and said, her voice not angry but dead-earnest, deadly serious, "You think you had it so bad in that private sanatorium that Daddy paid a thousand dollars a month to keep you in, do you? With the . . . bars and, well . . . treatments. Do you?" I said nothing, I was too astonished to speak. The sanatorium was never mentioned between the walls of the Glass House. Not once since my return home.

"Well, look at this then," she continued. "This is where Daddy had to stay." And shyly, almost tenderly, she held out a small photograph. Wordlessly I took it, astonished into muteness, blindness. My ears filled up with a sound like thundering waterfalls. Until then I had not known my father had been incarcerated in a crazy house just like his daughter. Me, the Dreamer. But the photograph. Ah, Mommy, I could have, save for certain details, seen that photograph with my eyes closed, sketched it with my own numb, blind fingertips.

It was a photograph of a large square room. The floor looked brown – linoleum, I suppose – and the walls and the ceiling the same, that funny dense sepia brown some photographs of the '40s have. Wire mesh and bars on the windows. And the beds, the narrow beds with the iron legs and spring mattresses visible above the iron frame, were lined up side by side.

A lone man stood by one of the wire mesh and barred windows looking out, smoking a cigarette, his feet bare. He wore a loose pyjama top, unbuttoned – his chest was concave – and baggy trousers without a belt (no belts, no sharps, no shoelaces, no fire-sticks). Some things remain a constant, I thought, forever unchangeable. His trousers were way too large for him. His head had been shaved. I wondered if he'd had a lobotomy.

There were many beds, row upon row, in the large square room. Perhaps fifty.

"It's a dorm," I said at last. "It's the Dorm."

"Yes, it is a dormitory," Clarice said, righteousness in her voice. "And see how many beds. See? Fifty, sixty? I don't know. I never counted. And that ugly brown! The dorm you were in had only twenty-one beds and a lot more light from that big wide window floor to ceiling –"

"Meshed and barred," I said.

"Floor to ceiling, a lot more light than the dormitory Daddy had to stay in and brown, brown, everything brown, the colour of crap! Your dorm had white curtains on the windows. And twenty-one beds. And if you really care to know – oh I know you're thinking you were so hard done by, just . . . just forced into . . . treatments – Daddy had shock treatments too!" And then she snatched the photograph from my hand and, in swirls of cigarette smoke, the smoke coiling around her wrists like bracelets, she left the room.

It was said. I thought, My pain fills a thimble; his fills an ocean.

But it was not so very different really. Not the way Clarice thought. Timothy rose and fell with the forty-nine or fifty-nine Others in a square room. Mine with the twenty Others in a round room. I slept in a narrow bed with iron legs on an iron frame and a thin mattress. I too took mass showers, varicose veins and sagging behinds and breasts and grey and auburn and jet-black, yellow and brown pubic hair all seemingly merging together into one huge wired tangle like an enormous Kurly Kate. There were thin bodies, emaciated bodies, fat bodies, hugely obese bodies, slender, shapely bodies; breasts like watermelons hanging below waists, high breasts, pendulous purple-veined breasts. The attendant in a grey uniform who ran the shower controls smoked a cigarette, lazily watching us, her eyelids half closed with the boredom of switching on hot sprays of water, then cold sprays. On-off, on-off.

I imagine Daddy had to take mass showers too, but I was a girl and fifteen years old and painfully shy and had never been seen naked since childhood by anyone before except the family doctor. Even the boy who touched me Downthere did it with his hands slipped into my panties, no hint of my flesh was revealed. Rising and falling with the fifty-nine Others. Rising and falling with the twenty Others.

He as I did must have listened to their moans, their strangled nightmares riding the endless oceans of nights where love only came, oh, oh so reluctant, to stroke a fevered brow, to slide a blessed needle filled with opiates into a vein to kill the dream rising. Love coming reluctant and weary on soft rubber-soled shoes, white-winged cap askew, flashlight beams probing like alien white eyes, like weapons. Who will hit? Who's violent tonight? Tie down! Tie down! Night nurses, some very kind but always cautious, wearily brushing a damp strand of hair out of a tired eye and, "There, there," sliding oh blessed needle filled with Opiate the Sandman into the blue vein, searching for it with the flashlight beam and always, always watching their backs.

I know Daddy's dreams must have been awful but I had dreams that rose up with emptied, gouged-out eyeholes and blood and fire pouring out of veins. Dreams with teeth. I had the mountain of tiny shoes.

The mountain of tiny shoes. In the end I think that may be why I ended up having shock treatments. My father's dream mountains might have been mountains of red sandstorms like walls of blood, or mountains of bombs, or blackened cities. Mine were of small empty shoes. Since I had been a minor, of course, I'd had no decision in the shock treatments but the doctors told my parents I did not seem to be improving very much and so shock therapy was advised. And agreed to.

It was true. I was despondent. In some ways it was easier being away from the Glass House. Curiously, I felt safer than I ever had before. I was surviving at last, though I kept remembering a fistful of grey ashes caught in my hand when I was six years old as I stood on the bluffs. Remembering that I had no truth, no self to call my own, since every truth I ever had was called lie, even after I was certain the soft flurry of grey ashes like dust caught in my hand was nothing more than ashes from burning leaves, smoking shrubbery. Even as I improved in some ways, ate a little more, gained five pounds, took to making baskets and knitting in O.T., under duress, I kept remembering the mountain of tiny shoes.

We'd had a subscription to *Life* magazine and even at five I could read, and although not a wildly wonderful reader I was not bad. Every week I thumbed through the copy of *Life* that came to our house and was left on the mail ledge.

One day I was looking as I always did at the large photographs and reading as best I could the print beneath. I came across a photograph that was absolutely magical. I blinked. I could not believe it! A huge mountain built not of stone, of jagged rock, but of tiny shoes, tiny shoes like little wood people's shoes. What wonders! A mountain of tiny shoes. But then the wonder faded. There was something, anyone could see, so very sad – and more – terrible, in the unearthliness of those tiny empty shoes.

My eyes found the text and made out the words "burned" and "gassed" and "hanged." The tiny shoes had belonged to the children who had been burned and gassed and hanged in the concentration camps. I had seen newsreels on our TV every Sunday night after dinner. This was my mountain of tiny shoes. My wonder. And it is to wonder. I felt hot. I shivered. Very slowly, very carefully, so as not to cause a page to rustle, so as not to disturb anything lying within the tomb of pages, I closed the magazine and put it back on the mail ledge.

Then I went up to my room and lay on the attic floor and watched the dust motes falling through the triangle of sunlit window like tiny white butterflies and thought of my tormented life in school. "If you are not of Us, you are of Them." I lay there until supper-time, when I sat among the lumps and shadows at the yellow Formica table and quietly ate.

Perhaps if it had ended there with a photograph. But for as long as I could remember, three streets over from our street, Fairfield Boulevard, there had been a small plaza with a small grocery store run by a man from Europe and his wife and a teenage son. The son, who was perhaps fourteen or fifteen, was bald because he had cancer and was receiving treatments for it. He did not go to school because of his cancer but helped out his father and mother in the store. Some of the kids made fun of him and called him "chrome dome" and "billiard-ball head."

The bully boys would put slugs in the Coke machine in the store and scatter the vegetables on the floor the boy had just washed and once rode around and around him in circles on their bicycles, calling him names, taunting him.

Under the photograph of the mountain of tiny empty shoes it had said the children whose shoes these had been were Jewish children. I had never really, not until I was five and saw that picture, connected the camps in Europe and the mass slaughter with the Jews. Even though at a very young age I'd seen parts of the War on television, the bodies piled in heaps, coiled thin like rope, seen thousands, millions of dead, like heaps of nylon stockings, corpses filling up pits, I never connected these dead, these bodies, with Jews.

I began to think of the neighbourhood women bending, smiling, hands dipping into pockets of blue or salmon-coloured housedresses, fishing out a dime and saying, "Go to the Jew-Joint," which was synonymous with Gyp-Joint. Any kid knows what a gyp is and knows that a gyp is not a good thing, not a nice thing, it is an undesirable. The neighbourhood women used these two words interchangeably when referring to the grocery store in the small plaza three streets over from ours.

The next time Clarice sent me with some money to the Gyp-Joint for a loaf of bread I couldn't – wouldn't – think too long or hard on the fact that my own mother also blithely spoke these words, smiling as she spoke them, smiling as all the mothers in our good, loving neighbourhood smiled at their children. Smiling with kerchiefs wrapped around their freshly permed hair, permed and dried under the pink hair dryers at Fran's Hair Salon in the same plaza the Gyp-Joint-Jew-Joint was in.

The coins were sweaty in the palm of my hand when I went into the grocery store. The teenage boy was there hosing down the vegetables – lettuce, tomatoes, cucumbers, bunches of radishes. I wondered how to find voice. It was the first time I had ever formally met a Jew, now that I knew he was one. I asked the grocer's boy in a small, polite voice for a loaf of WonderBread. Every Saturday morning on "Howdy Dowdy" they extolled the virtues of Wonder-Bread. Clarabell tooted his horn over it and Buffalo Bob loved it as much as he loved all those boxed and cellophaned Twinkies. The boy got it for me and went over to the cash register. I slid my money across the counter, first wiping the dampness of the coins from my hands on my sunsuit. Scuffing my white sandals against the wooden floor. I looked down at my feet.

And while he was packaging the WonderBread for me in a brown paper bag, when I was sure he wasn't looking, I looked down at his feet too.

When I was six I buried some grey ashes, no doubt from a burning pile of raked leaves, in sun-warmed white sand

and then, by the time I was fifteen, the blue winter set in, bluer than blue, you could see the ribbons of God on Catholic schoolgirls' slips even in the dark bleeding into Dark, it was all so blue, the Pieta bleeding, bleeding, and God was a relentless Eater just as the Earth was. The delicately painted lips of the neighbourhood women. Clarice's finely drawn mouth. That hot summer day when Clarice — her sweet-shaped mouth twisted into ugliness — and hatred? Yes, I am sure of that. How not hatred and me buried in a bloodied coffin of used sanitary napkins?

But the shock treatments. Oh how Daddy and I could have talked about that. As far as I know he'd never discussed them with a living soul. Not even Clarice. He had it worse than I did, of course. By the time I got around to having them in the early '60s they used a drug to put you under, a needle slid into a vein, but not before they strapped you down, wrists and ankles, to prevent broken bones, and then jammed the black rubber gag into your mouth. My electrodes went on both sides of my head, on both throbbing temples. I only had to bear, sweat through watching the doctor turn the dial up on the black shock box before I lost consciousness.

Daddy's electrodes also went on both temples, but he had no drug slid into his vein, he did not lose consciousness, not until that final exploding moment when the fire-sparks filled up his brain.

Afterwards, of course, the headaches were mind-boggling, skull-shattering, mind-obliterating. Your whole head, every bone in it, hurt so badly that you could not bear for your teeth attached to screaming jawbone to touch even lightly together, and the only thing you could eat for two days after a shock treatment was crackers soaked in milk.

For the pain of the headaches after the shock treatments one was given two Aspirins every four hours or as the doctor thought needed.

And perhaps, like myself, Daddy had to watch and listen to the poor helpless insulin-shock patients moan and sweat and groan and call out imploringly like crazed falling-down drunks for sweet juice, for sweets, for candy. It was a debate at the sanatorium I resided in as to which was worse – electric shock spewing fire through brain cells, cresting and rippling through cerebral ridges, or the soft white-soled nurses silently walking towards someone on the ward with a needle loaded with deadly moaning sweating insulin. Nickel and dime and quarter bets were made on this subject in the Day Room over dully played card and cribbage games or in the tub rooms, one bather betting with the bather beside them in the next tub.

There was a man I knew who was lobotomized because he had been suicidal. I felt the soft, fleshy pulsing spots on both sides of his head where the bits of skull had been taken away. He guided my fingers gently, wordlessly, to his broken, ruined head and I wept for his innocence. Later he had thanked the doctors who performed the operation, thanked them in a monotone, the only voice they'd left him.

Muted and bound they drift through my skull like mists, like fog, in eerie vapours. Their screams my screams.

There was a time when the Bone-Man ran free. Or very nearly. The Bone-Man was a resident at the sanatorium I was in, not the hospital Daddy was in.

The Bone-Man was very old, although some at the sanatorium said he might not be as old as he looked since he'd had over a hundred shock treatments from Chief Deadbolts, and that could age a man. Standing in line for night meds in our nighties and housecoats and worn slippers we'd whisper about the Bone-Man and nod sagely. He was legend around the place. He'd been there so long, most of the Staff had forgotten his name and he was simply known by the number of his ward and dormitory and the position of his bed by number-4 closet. Name: Ward A-3, Bed By Number-4 Closet.

For reasons no one understood (not even Staff, it was rumoured) no one knew why Chief Deadbolts kept putting the Bone-Man on the shock list even after over one hundred shock treatments. Some whispered it had been more like a hundred and twenty.

"How can he be alive any more is what I want to know?" John the Fire-Thrower said one afternoon as he casually found something in his nose when we were sunning in the lawn chairs flanked by pterodactyls.

He was called the Bone-Man because he was so very frail, thin as dust. His bones showed through his skin. His hair was a shock of electric white. His eyes were an almost colourless blue, azure. All the electricity shooting through his skull all those years had burned all the colour and life from his eyes.

The shock treatments were given in a huge amphitheatre where ninety or more of us sat at a time with our Keepers, waiting to be led two by two through the little black door far below the high curved benches we sat on. The walls were green. The little door was jet-black and without a door-knob. One was taken to the green amphitheatre with a Keeper through an underground series of hot shadowed hallways filled with all kinds of piping, deep in the bowels of the sanatorium. Hardly anyone ever spoke on the journey through the twisting underground to the amphitheatre.

Once, on an ordinary enough Shock Shop day, about ninety of us as usual were waiting on the curved benches with our Keepers, our faces ghastly under the green shadows cast by the green room, our eyes locked on the knobless black door far below. The Bone-Man was there with his Keeper, a big, meaty red-faced blond man who smoked a cigarette. Helene was there, dancing along the curved benches, her dark beautiful eyes blank, her usually expressive weaving arms dead and stiff as two pieces of wood.

"Helene, be still! Helene, sit down! Do I have to tie you down! Put you in a Quiet Room?" Her blue-aproned Keeper kept threatening but Helene was beyond hearing, beyond words. It was only her second shock treatment.

I was sitting beside the boy with the copper hair and burns the size of nickels on his palms. He was wringing his hands together as he always did, as if to wash away the scars of the burns, as if to make them vanish, go back into his palms, making them whole again. He was cursing softly beneath his breath. There were a few whimpering sounds, sometimes now and again a jagged sob. But mostly just a-waiting. A holding of breath. Even the blood in our veins waited, seemed to stop, held suspended, frozen.

Things were humming along pretty much as usual in the Shock Factory, people being processed two by two behind the knobless black door, when suddenly a wild cry leaped out into the room, creating a din within the cavernous green walls of the amphitheatre. Everyone's necks snapped to, whipping round. No one ever made a sound louder than a strangled sob in the Shock Factory. It was not done. It was part of the etiquette. The amphitheatre by virtue of its very roundness, its high ceilings, the green, cavernous spaces of it and how it caused footfalls to become muted, was, well, sacrosanct.

And yet someone had cried out, had protested in a wild, angry cry. We stared. It was the Bone-Man, all eighty pounds of him on his feet, his white hair like a white lick of flame, with all that sparking electricity that had filled him all these years overflowing in him now. He was running, his Keeper, lazing with his Rothmans having momentarily shifted his gaze, and the Bone-Man was running, flaming-white and screaming, "NOT AGAIN! NOT AGAIN! I WON'T HAVE IT!"

The beefy Keeper was on his feet, flinging away his cig-arette, muttering, "Shit!" and on strong feet running after the Bone-Man, who was not made of dust now but of white flame. One by one those of us awaiting our turn in the Shock Shop behind the knobless black door rose to our feet and then it began. A cheer here, a cheer there, and then a great rolling, howling cheer went up and up and along with it a wild stomping of feet. The men whistled, fists raised, women too raising fists like champion prizefighters in a ring, winning the gold cup, and still the Bone-Man ran on, running wildly in circles around the room, in confusion, seeking out the door, his Keeper gaining but still behind.

"I WILL NOT HAVE IT! NEVER AGAIN! I WILL NOT HAVE IT!"

Sheet lightning!

"Impossible to stop him now!" crowed Fats, his arms straining and righting invisible two-ton stone pillars, beard wild, Sampson glaring and alive.

Helene's arms were weaving again to a soaring cacophony of sound only she could hear, a frenzied, beautiful poetry. The Keepers were all on their feet, aprons twisting, keys clanging and clattering. Their hands, snatching out crazy and blind, grabbing for wrists, arms, ankles, legs, were frantic, lost. The boy with the copper hair and purple nickel burns all over his hands and a sabre carved into his back turned to me and picked me up and spun me around and around, shouting out triumphantly, "Oh girlie! Oh girlie!"

The emergency bell rang an alarm. The voice of Hell.

"NEVERNEVERNEVERFUCKINGNEVERAGAIN! I WON'T HAVE IT!" Sheet lightning storms. The whole amphitheatre lit up by the Bone-Man's white brilliance. And the Keeper, all two hundred and fifty pounds of him, staggered, then regained his footing, righted himself, and wrapped a ham of a hand around the Bone-Man's toothpick of an ankle and brought him crashing down to his tiny pinpoints of knees.

Silence.

Except for a sobbing.

The Bone-Man's sobbing and breathless panting.

In ones, then twos and threes, slowly we sat down again on the curved benches, the Keepers calming, keys settling at aproned waists, quieting. Only a shattered sobbing broke the still and waiting air of the amphitheatre, broke our still and waiting hearts.

16.

TIMOTHY DREAMS.

He dreams he is an architect and he builds beautiful buildings, homes that are so fine, so perfect that they seem sprung from the Earth's core itself, the Earth's very centre, sprung right out of Rhea's soul and moulded by genius hands. Sunlight streams, light-gold clouds, through the windows of the homes he builds and bounces off the high-hipped roofs. Every brick, every bit of mortar is perfect, a pure truth in his buildings. He dreams of leaning over a draughting table and drawing razor-thin lines in black ink that will become these homes, become brick and wood and shingle and joist and nail and glass pane.

A ghost of a smile flickers on the winter-white face lying on the crisp pillow on the raft bed, but there is no one there to see it. The banks of flowers on the windowsills and bedside tables freshly put there by Dinah and Rachel that morning don't care. But a fat blind worm uncoils in a lazy stretch of white frost and slithers across Timothy's face.

The ghost of a smile flattens into coma. Timothy is no longer dreaming, not the good dreaming in this Place of Not (for it is all dream now), he is awake as awake as the Un-Dead and Buried can be and floating in a salty pond of despair. A lake of tears. Like Alice. Six-foot white worm sliding away, blind to all but pulse and some long-ago remembered need of – something.

Timothy had planned to become an architect. He was going to go on from high school to university and study to become an architect, but he remembers walking down King Street on a freezing-cold winter day, people looking like shadows, like spirits scurrying along. He was walking along King Street and saw the banner with RECRUITING CENTRE written on it in black print and it was War – 1940. He remembers Winston Churchill's voice ringing out over the radio and Mother's teacup trembling in her lap and the boys marching, hundreds and hundreds of boys, boys marching in row after row, singing, *Over there, over there* . . .

The War changed all that for him; his dreams of becoming an architect.

The lake of tears grows wider, deeper. Instead of becoming an architect he joined the RCAF and came home not who he had once been somehow. He was never sure quite how he was not the same. Although an extremely intelligent man, he was not a self-examining man. That kind of self-ness frightened him. It was only like – like he had once been a whole smooth-ticking clock, understanding the

147

flow of time and chiming exactly on the hour, but after the War and after the Hospital it was like a coil, a spring, some mechanism inside the once smooth-ticking clock was missing. His understanding of time became confused. A blankness began to fill his brain.

Did time jerk as on a clock face, move in spasms, did it flow fluid like water? Like liquid? Was it linear? A dot simply to a dot? But it isn't really a clock that he means. He means him. The blankness filling his brain is not just Time. He knows that. Time in him is missing and with it other parts of him are missing, missing with minutes that have fallen in torrents, in floods, whole thundering waterfalls, and he is somehow filled with these blanks where that smooth-flowing had once been.

His dreams were smoke, like the smoke that spiralled over all the burned-out, blackened cities of Europe. The smoulderings over desert, seas. The smoke that rose in the streets over the buildings into the screaming sky during the fire-bombings of London. The smoke that rose out of mass crematoriums filled with the charred bones of the Jews and the gypsies, and the homosexuals and the mad. Smoke and corpses.

He married Clarice and had children, one right after the other, three or four or five, he thinks, or it seems one right after the other, and there was the need for money with a family and no time for dreams of school and architecture and drawing and building beautiful homes.

Smoke and stinking corpses.

He had been sickly as a small boy, and an intelligent boy. Spending much of his time in bed he read books far beyond his age but not beyond his ken and he took to drawing. He drew well, very well. He drew faces, caricatures, animals, illustrations from books. But what he liked drawing best were buildings. Houses. His houses. His mother was worried, he was so frail and polio crawled the streets in the summers and so he supposed that was when she replied to the advertisement in the *Telegram* and wrote the man he came to call Uncle Ned, who owned a farm up north.

Dear Mother practically begged the man to take on her sickly five-year-old boy as a "helper" around the farm, stating that although he was very young he was obedient and worked hard and followed instructions well and was very bright. Uncle Ned had been searching for hands for his farm, offering room and board but no pay. He could not pay the men.

He supposed Mother thought the farmer would think her mad asking him to take on a five-year-old boy, and a sickly boy at that, but Mother had ended her letter, written in blue ink on her crinkly white and gold-embossed personal notepaper, in her elegant hand: *It is just that he is so frail and a summer away in the country would toughen him and I worry so and I love him so*. Amazingly, the farmer wrote back and said the boy could come, but he would have to pull his weight.

That was how it began, Uncle Ned and the farm and a horse called Old Bob and the hired men and the swim hole. Thirteen summers, summer to summer from the time he was five until he was eighteen years old Timothy worked Uncle Ned's farm and loved Old Bob and jawed with the hired hands and snuck his first smoke out behind the barn at seven. He did the mowing and haying and picking and planting and the hundred other things hired hands did.

But still he read and still he drew and who could have known what would happen that last summer? And then it was King Street in winter and 1940 and War and he never went back to the farm again. Not even to visit Uncle Ned, whom he had come to love and who lived a very long time after Timothy's last summer on the farm.

Nope, that last summer with what happened at the farm, and how he could never forget it, and then the War, everything went up in flame and smoke. So instead of becoming an architect he took his good mind and, hat in hand, went to the Bell Telephone Company, and told them he could draw the underground cables for them. And that was that. Over the years, of course, his position advanced. He was a very intelligent man but younger university-educated men kept coming up through the ranks as the years went by and sailed past him, even though by that time he was working with computers way back in the beginnings of computers being used in workplaces, but that was just the way things were. That's life, guys and dolls, he used to tell his children.

At the end of it all, his position paid well and he made some shrewd investments in good solid stocks but, instead of discussing the elegant lines of buildings or vaulted ceilings or sliding walls, he would stand around the water cooler with Bell men who had not been sickly children and had not read into the night until their eyes burned raw and red. He read history, all the history books he could lay his hands on, and mythology and theology and poetry. And war novels. Timothy drowning in the lake of tears thinks, Well, fooled them, didn't I?

The Bell men around the water cooler. Talked sports and politics with them just like they expected, he thinks. Never opened my mouth about houses that rose up through the clouds, buildings that were as bright and airy as sky and sunlight, roof spires that touched stars. Never opened my mouth about Idat or Icarus or Cerebus or the aeries or wars fought in the sixth century or talked about the volumes of poetry tucked away in the boxes in the attic at that one house I did build. The one house I designed, drew myself – though I'd never been taught how to draw a house, or how to be an architect – and I drew it well, built it myself, with my own hands and no one else's hands from the ground up. Out of Rhea my House of Glass sprung.

Over the years there had been a few close men friends but none that read as he did, a habit that was lifelong, and none that was Ian Glass, dead on the Rock of Gibraltar in '42. He supposes for all the talking he did he hardly talked at all about anything that he thought about. Really thought about. He talked well, a good game of politics and sports, and laughed often, but did not go for long liquid lunches with the Bell men who did, or feel easy with their some-times off-colour jokes. Rather he'd sit at his desk and eat the lunch that Clarice had prepared for him from a brown paper bag and read his latest history book. Or the speeches of Winston Churchill. A book on Ghandi. The words of Thackeray. Or biographies of famous heads of state, presi-dents and princes, kings and queens, and famous generals and field marshals. Read books on the Civil War in the States, weeping over the men caged behind twisted barbed wire in the American-style concentration camp, Andersonville.

Been drunk only once in his life, on a leave in London during the War with some of the other Fly Boys and the parrots and the monkeys, the little spider monkey Reginald riding on Timothy's shoulder, and wild cats and old yellow dogs going nuts as they rode the wrong way on the up and then the down escalator, the parrots taking vivid-painted wing up into the high-domed ceiling, the monkeys chittering with insane joy, and the cats a-yowling, tails flicking as if on a great hunt, drunk on the rye whiskey that had been set out for them in saucers on the bartop by the barkeep.

Timothy is standing on boards. Cheap blond-wood boards. Boards that cover muck. It is not the lush countryside of Scarborough he moved into back in '47, the tricky, jerking clock hand has shifted into the late '50s when the new "Creative Developments" are springing up everywhere. He stands here now; time is a tunnel and he has flowed through it. His eyes are filled with pain as he watches the tall stately trees being torn from the earth and every last flower and bit of shrubbery and blade of grass wrenched out to make way for more tearing up and for building-machines and tar and asphalt and cement and white curbs and brick bungalows, either salmon-pink or grey brick with white cornerstones, with the long, low red- or green- or grey-shingled roofs, endless faces reflected in a multitude of mirrors.

These new "Creative Developments" had kitchen nooks and laundry rooms and recreation rooms with fake wood panelling and red bar lights flickering under plastic shades and blue-and-grey-tiled rec-room floors and pool tables and a TV alcove and bar stools and long arborite bars in every bungalow. He can smell the rain and the muck. This was after all vegetation had been uprooted and before the streets and driveways. The people who lived in the long low grey or salmon-pink bungalows walked these blond boards over seas of muck to work and school and grocery shopping or when visiting at one another's bungalow homes with identical red bar lights and fake wood panelling and breakfast nooks.

He remembers that one of his girls, Number-Two Daughter, the Dreamer, is abysmally poor in math, a nightmare of incomprehension. They have sent her to math tutors. She has gone through three in all. She has managed to finish them all off into sobbing, keening, blubbering pools before they could even begin to drill one bit of math into her head.

Timothy thinks of this now as he stands in the rain on the cheap blond boards laid end to end. He is looking at the fourth and last math tutor's house. A smallish, low grey bungalow without a single tree or blade of grass around it. He walks up to the door of the math tutor's house, carefully picking his way over the boards slippery with rain, muck edging slick over the edges, and he steps inside.

He sees the frazzled tutor, a young man in his mid-twenties with bluish stubble on his cheeks and thick black horn-rimmed eyeglasses, sitting at a green card table in the rec room with the grey-and-blue-tiled floor. The Dreamer sits opposite him, the math textbooks spread out between them on the table.

The Dreamer is dreaming with her eyes wide open the way she always does. The tutor is gesturing with a pencil, driving a point home on the textbook page regarding a particular algebra equation. The Dreamer's green eyes glaze over as she drifts further away into her dreaming. The rain pounds steadily against the panes of the squat basement windows. The tutor taps his pencil frantically. The Dreamer's white hair is a cloud of angel hair over her green eyes, over her rainbowing dreams.

They cannot see him. The math tutor and the Dreamer. It is his coma, his Alzheimer's, his Place of Not.

Timothy wants to scream: Oh what he could have wrought, what homes he could have built, and he stands there and listens to the rain drilling into his skull, for there are no strong tree limbs or leaves to break the steady falling of the rain.

He thinks of the columns, the portcullis gates, the intricate trellises he had planned to have at the entranceway of the driveways to homes with rich green vines climbing the trellis. Or bunches of purple grapes on wiry dark-green vines on either side of the drive, gardens with graceful, curved benches and vibrant-yellow and crimson-red flowers springing up along glittering stone pathways like gifts.

Just then he sees a smile on the Dreamer's lips, not hidden at all, but blooming like a garden flower. He does not understand it, but he loves her very much just then. She is enough to drive anyone crazy with her dreaming green eyes, eyes that are veiled like purple dusk, like smoke is covering them. She is filled with secrets. He knows this and he thinks that he alone in the Glass Family understands this.

He does not want to know them.

As a child she banged her head monotonously against walls and floors, for hours, singing tunelessly. Never mournfully, never with sadness, no, only note after tuneless note, singing and singing in a humming drone, and beating her head until lumps sprang up like mushrooms on her skull and blood trickled in thin red rivers down through her white hair. It sorrowed him but, in the end, more than sorrow or puzzlement, there was his anger.

How dare she be strange, different! After all, he fought a War and he built a good house and grew good gardens and he provided well for his family and he wants rightness and order and not cobwebbed veils drawn over eyes or smiles hidden in smoke. But looking at her now, at this moment, he loves her and he isn't sure why.

And then he sees muck sliding through the casements of the low basement windows, sliding down the carefully moulded fake wood panelling, the rain drilling like nails into his head. Sliding down the pale-grey fake wood panelling and onto the blue and grey squares of tile. And the small smile in his heart is gone, and the love has gone thin and vaporous as the smoke of her smile.

He thinks about the scores of guidance counsellors, the long, drawn-out meetings with teachers; the IQ tests, the teachers always frowning on Parents Night when he and Clarice go into the Dreamer's classrooms. *Not like the other girls.*

Maybe, maybe that's why he likes to sit with her in the garden. She is so quiet, so impenetrable and quiet. She never asks for anything, anything at all. The others asked. He remembers shouting at Rachel, once, "Look at that child, happy as a clam with a simple rope!" He was speaking of the Dreamer when Rachel had complained about not getting what she wanted for her Easter gift. And he remembers now – quick, quick before he forgets for he is flowing back back through the tunnel of time to the Underworld, to the Place of Not – he remembers how the whole family, Dinah and Lillian and Rachel and Clarice and himself, looked uneasily out the kitchen window at the Dreamer standing on the front lawn beside the towering maple trees, spinning her rope, just spinning – as she would spin it like that for hours, all day into the night, just spinning and staring – and then they all looked away and silence fell over the room.

Fast, fast he is falling into Born-Not but his last thoughts are these: I would have been a damn good architect. Why did that last summer on the farm have to happen? Old Bob, Old Bob – and then there is nothing. A long, long time of Nothing.

17.

"I COULD HAVE lied about it, I suppose," I tell The Kid as we walk home from the cheap local grocery store, The Kid dragging the bundle-buggy filled with groceries behind him up the hill to our house.

"You shoulda, Mom," says The Kid. "I sure would have. You got shit for it."

Sure did, I think. From the Sunnydale Staff, and indignation from The Sisters Three. But that was months ago.

It is mid-spring now. A mild day, sunny, warm, breezy. For four days Daddy has lain in exactly the same position. Not so much as a finger-twitch. A breath expelled through nostril or mouth that has force enough to indicate that he is alive at all. Boy, what I wouldn't give to pump a forty-ouncer of scotch into Daddy's veins right now. The nurses turn him so he won't get bedsores. His hands are claws against the white bedsheets, nails dug into the blinding white, and frozen as if rigor mortis has set in.

If I held my compact mirror up to him, would his breath come steaming white fog? Would his ghosts come white and dancing out? I've always known my father had more ghosts than most men. All the dead boys he wanted to come smiling and marching home, wounded perhaps, but smiling and marching and coming home all the same.

May 8th, 1945, VE-Day. I had read about it. People draped themselves from lampposts and crouched on building ledges, they danced in the streets and leaned out of all the office-building windows, shouting and waving and cheering. Strangers embraced and kissed one another on streetcars and on street corners. The train and bus stations were filled with tears and laughter and incredulity when it was all over Over There, truly over, and they came marching home with ribbons on their chests and bands playing. But Ian Glass was dead on Gibraltar in '42, and he did not smile and march and no band beat on for him. Timothy Glass's best friend in the whole damn War, in the whole damn world.

And the other ghosts. The hospital ghosts. He must carry them inside him, just as I do.

Still, I wouldn't have lied. Not about the scotch. And I tell this to The Kid now.

"But why, Mom? You caught hell for it."

"Because he was – he is – a grown-up. Sixty-nine years old, for godssake, and he had a right to a drink. Drinking is not prohibited in nursing homes. They are not hospitals. And some of the old guys in there did drink. A few of the old women did too. They got dirty looks from Staff but drank all the same."

"I guess," The Kid says in misery.

That past winter when Daddy was still in Sunnydale I had taken to sneaking bottles of scotch into him in my oversized handbag. Ballantine's. That's what he always used to drink, every night after work from a stubby glass as he sat in the Windsor chair in front of the fireplace, in winter the fire burning in the black grate.

So I began to smuggle it into him. Like guilty children we giggled in his room as we poured the scotch into the paper Dixie cups from the colourless plastic dispenser in the bathroom. He'd sit on the edge of his bed and close his eyes and drink deep of it. I'd sit on a stiff-backed chair, which I'd drawn up to his bed, and smoke with the bureau drawer beside me open, the bureau drawer where I'd put the ashtray I carried in my purse so that if a nurse or aide happened to come in I could quick drop the butt into the ashtray and slide the drawer closed.

His roommate was gone then. He had died. Daddy said he was really sorry about that but now at least he wouldn't have his chocolates stolen any more and again we laughed like guilty children and poured more scotch into our paper Dixie cups. We weren't being callous. Institutions do that to you. Put skins on you. It is called survival.

The scotch helped him, it really did. His glass and wire and porcelain limbs loosened, became almost flesh and blood again. He'd smile. He wasn't talking coherent English any more, garbled, mysterious anagrams, word puzzles, fractured syntax, but if I listened very carefully, more often than not I could follow what he was saying. As the scotch began to work its mellow magic Daddy would say, "Swim up couple of sheets for me. One's good." That was pretty easy. I knew he wanted me to read to him. And I would.

I don't know how much he understood of what I read to him from the condensed *Reader's Digest*s provided by the scant Sunnydale Library or the one book he most often would press into my hands, *The Gathering Storm*. As I read he'd drink and nod, sometimes smile or murmur, and, eventually well-liquored, as I read Winston Churchill's valiant words he'd fall asleep, the Dixie cup tilted forward on his chest and dribbling scotch onto his blue jogging top.

Gently I'd remove the paper cup from those wondrous loose flesh-and-blood fingers, rinse it out in the bathroom sink, and crumple it up into a ball and throw it into the wastebasket, for the benefit of Staff Sniffers.

We passed quite a few agreeable winter afternoons in this way, considering where we were and considering his condition. The snow falling thickly beyond his window, double-spun sheets like damask tablecloths, the sky beaten metal, the lamplight in his room spilling over *The Gathering Storm* in a golden pool, and my voice labouring on and on forever, it seemed, for he never tired of the words, whatever he understood. Spinning white snow, Dixie cups refilled again and again with the amber liquid, and Daddy sometimes would shake his head and smile, saying only, "Oh, Winnie, Winnie."

My eyes would rise from the black printed words to the jagged grey piece of wood on the wall above his bed, to the thick white paint strokes: Flight Squadron Number 517.

The War, I thought, thinking of the tiny black-and-white photographs in the ancient album, the War, from the beginning of it for him, in 1940, to now – to this, his ending (the beginning of his ending? imminent?). The War for Timothy Glass has been everything.

And somehow my war too. Always. Outside, the snow fell steadily, and I'd puzzle over that thought in the overwarm room in the golden lamplight, the long winter shadows leaping dark into the room. My war too. It had always been so. From the time memory begins recording, coding. Mine. His War memories were – are – somehow mine.

The summer nights in the gardens. Often there was only the silence and the rising and falling of the red cigarette tip in the black night. But other times he would talk, talk on and on. Chain-smoking always, ashes falling steadily as snow-flakes, sometimes drinking a cocktail but he wasn't ever drunk. He only drank a single scotch and soda, never more than two, the talk spilling out into the hot night air, fireflies flitting and darting, lighting his words. I remember some-times words would tear out of him like wind, at other times burst out like musical notes, high and spiralling. Sometimes I remember the words coming out like great angry beasts torn from his body.

But what could he have told me? I was very young. Two, three, maybe four. I crouched beside his lawn chair for hours at a time without moving, just listening if not comprehending much of it. Sometimes he'd stop suddenly and accuse me of dreaming, but soft, soft, no anger in it. "Beautiful Dreamer, wake unto me," he'd sing to me, lifting me up into his lap and sometimes he'd cry into my soft white hair. He would tell me it was like spun glass, like the white hair of the angel we would put atop the Christmas tree every year.

"Beautiful Dreamer, when will you wake?" Then he'd set me down on the grass again by the grape arbour and his words would again begin and the cigarettes lit up one after the other, quick and darting as the fireflies' white lights, his red lights.

The talking of the War in this way stopped when I was perhaps four, certainly no older than five. How can I remember it then? I recall no exact sentences, at least I think not. God whispering. That. I remember that, and something about a sliver of a moon being God's eyelash. And bombs. Bombs and bombs. Hundreds, thousands. And the rest?

I know what I know. Maybe it's like the opium, what Daddy once said about the opium. *Opium does that. It knows what it knows.* I know I was born with a difference, but it isn't a difference that can be defined by anyone, not even doctors of psychiatry. So you could say it was like something flowed between us in the gardens and allowed his words to run into me, into my veins, into my bloodstream, like the opium had flowed into him.

I know what I know.

It isn't just looking at all the photographs recently, examining them again and again. I know the words behind many of the photographs with just the briefest of glances, the stories, the faces, the valiant songs that were stopped mid-note in crashing black seas as night fell and another drowned. I can hear the screams when a plane began plummeting downward in flames.

One of the nurses found the bottle of Ballantine's in Daddy's bureau drawer as she was rummaging through it and a big meeting was held. Several nurses were there and the social worker and myself and The Sisters Three. The scotch, of course, was confiscated.

"Who gave him the scotch?" came the steely Staffer's voice. "Which one?"

There was silence for a long moment. The Sisters Three looked indignant, astonished. And then I spoke. "I did," I said.

I was given a good verbal thrashing for that by the Staff.

"Then at least give him his bloody Haldol," I said. "Every time he asks for it or I ask for him, you never give it. Not once! It is prescribed by his doctor. I know that. The doctor said so. Read his chart, can't you? Maybe if you gave him some of the damn Haldol, I wouldn't have to bring him the damn scotch."

"He receives the Haldol when the Staff thinks it necessary and only then," Steel Voice Two or Three said. All-Staff Voice in a whirring blender.

Silence.

The meeting adjourned.

The Sisters Three enraged.

With me.

As a small child I was terrified of any loud noise. I was most especially frightened by the loud and furious sound of thunderstorms. I remember my father would hold me in his arms up to the big living-room picture window when a storm came rumbling malevolently across the sky. Lightning would be dancing in white zigzags like handmaidens, attendants to the bigger show, and Daddy would hold me there to look out at it, to look straight into the evil-eye so I would get over my terror of loud sounds. A cigarette glued to his lips, he'd say, "Look, look, there's God whispering and he can't hurt you now."

I'd scream and scream.

Clarice's voice would come in, banal in the background, "Oh, Timothy, just tell her that's God moving His furniture around. That's what I thought when I was a child. That shouldn't scare a flea."

My father's face immobile, not turning to answer or acknowledge my mother, cigarette glued to mouth corner, eyes frozen to the boiling black sky lit by white fire, and I would quiet out of my terror with the pure truth of what he had spoken. God *was* whispering and the bombs fell by the hundreds, by the thousands, the black rain, and I could hear God whispering and my father could hear Him whispering, even if Clarice chattering in the background and The Sisters Three playing Chinese checkers on the ashes of roses carpet could not.

My father was taller than God. Once, I asked him to throw a handful of blue stars up into the sky and I am not sure that he did not.

His silence filled whole rooms.

Long ago my father called me into his opium dream and into his desert and his War and I had come, my eyeballs already peeled back at birth, skinned like two grapes and filled with All-Sight.

I know what I know.

18.

TIMOTHY SHIVERS WITH dizziness. It is all tumbling by so fast now, the memories, the travelling, a mad carousel gone out of control, spinning round faster and faster, the painted pony he rides heaving and snorting. The girls. The Glass girls. He always called them that, his five Glass girls. He has a wife – no, had – Clarice was her name, and she bought breasts and then she died and he had daughters, four.

Mother, he asks, why didn't you tell me more about little girls, about women? Never could do a damn thing with them once they started – growing. You should have said. Something.

The carousel spins, the painted red and gold pony prances, its blue nostrils flare and there is Princess, sixteen years old and gorgeous, didn't all the aunts and uncles and neighbours say the very same thing? Princess in her snow-white bathing suit with the low V-neck, her dark-brown hair with auburn highlights fashioned into a pageboy, riding her softly curved tanned shoulders like waves, her shapely legs made golden by the sun. She is sunning herself on the glittering pink and white rocks by the tea-rose garden, her smile radiant, her fingers elegant and golden as her legs, her nails perfectly manicured and polished to a bright-red sheen, long and pointed gracefully at the tips.

Faster, faster it spins, the memory, the leaping painted pony, the other carousel ponies prancing, prancing, and he sees she is wearing a ring. It flashes in the sun bright as a star. He remembers that summer day, Princess the Beauty. He took a snapshot of her sunning on the rocks by the tea roses – pink the roses were and in bunches of white, white and delicate as snowflakes, as clouds. He snapped the photograph because she looked so beautiful and she wanted a picture of herself wearing her new ring.

Rings cascade out of drawers and whirl like bright shining moons past the spinning carousel. Next week it would be another ring, another boy pinned to her and head over heels in love with her. Boyfriends; she had them by the dozens. Most of the boys he liked well enough but he always worried, Princess always so eager to grow up. Come to think of it she never really was a child at all, whereas the Dreamer . . .

Never mind.

Princess, he loved her, adored her, her quick mind, her good looks. He was so proud to have such a fine-looking, clever daughter, so proud that neighbours would stop him on the street and say, "That daughter of yours sure is a beauty." He never doubted which daughter they meant.

But he worried.

He left the raising of the girls to Clarice. What did he know about little girls growing into bigger girls? He worried and worried, Princess dating boys years older than herself and going to cocktail bars when she was sixteen. Even fourteen! She wanted a car, a snazzy little canary-yellow sports car, when she was seventeen years old and got it too! Once, so maddened with worry – no, no, stop spinning, please . . . please. But the memories fly and the painted pony rides and he sees it though he does not want to see it at all. Princess is fourteen years old and he is standing over her and beating her with a curtain rod and she is howling, howling, he who never raised a hand to any of his children in his life. She was fourteen and he awoke and heard her coming home way past one, nearly two, damn near three in the morning! As he angrily met her in the hallway, his face rumpled with sleep, wearing his dressing gown, her purse fell open. A dozen swizzle sticks fell out, green, yellow, red, pink, blue. She'd been out with that university man again. Timothy went crazy. Fourteen and drinking in bars with a university man and, if that, then what? He beat and beat her with a curtain rod, beat her until red welts were raised on her tender, soft skin, her arms, her legs, and she howled.

He never laid a hand on her again. Oh he is sorry, sorry as sorry. Is that why he is in the Inferno? For beating Princess, his Rachel, that night?

Now the Dreamer, you never had to even lay so much as a fingertip on her to get her to do whatever you asked. A raised voice and she would go into spasms of abject weeping; sometimes worse: fits of terror. There was no other way to describe it. And she would never say, not once, never, what terrified her so. She was afraid of odd things. The fingers of gloves, other things, he knew not what. Well, it fit that she acted odd. She was an odd-looking child.

He'll never forget the Dreamer on her first day born, snow-white hair and enormous eyes with snow-white eyelashes and a wrinkled brow. He swears she was born frowning. She was not a baby people cooed over or said was cute and pretty, like they did Princess and the twins. The twins were cute as two bugs in a rug. But the Dreamer was — well, even if she was his own, he had to admit — odd-looking. Not ugly. Not that, no.

As a teenager, she didn't have boyfriends. She dressed all in black like some beatnik, like that stupid Maynard Krebs on "The Many Loves of Dobie Gillis," and read Kierkegaard and Richard Wright and J. D. Salinger, who Clarice said wrote filth, pure filth. She had posters on her bedroom walls, not of rock and roll stars or teenage movie heartthrobs but one of Gertrude Stein with her lesbian lover, Alice B. something, Stein sitting on the edge of a fountain glaring out at the world. She had another poster, of the Lunts (the Lunts, for godssake), and a black-and-white postcard of James Baldwin and a photograph cut out of a magazine of Ayn Rand wearing a gold brooch shaped into a dollar sign.

She listened to jazz records — Miles Davis and Duke Ellington — when all the other teenagers were dancing to rock and roll. Every night jazz music blasted down through the house from high up within the attic eaves.

She had no friends. He knew she was extremely sensitive, shy; he himself, well, he had been that way as a boy, but you had to cope, overcome things like that. He bought her the book *The Power of Positive Thinking* by Norman Vincent Peale that last bad year, the year they had to send her away. He would bet every dollar he ever had that she never even opened it. That last bad year, the Dreamer's fifteenth year, he and Clarice tried everything.

The Dreamer screaming and rocking, rocking and screaming all day and night, and slicing herself up with hairpins, razors, and bits of glass, and burning herself with lit cigarettes. She said the winter was blue, all blue, everything was blue. Just blue. Clarice said, "She reads too much, she thinks too much, and she's too sensitive, gets ideas, and she never eats. She doesn't eat enough to keep a bird alive or drink her juice in the morning, never, ever drinks her damn juice, no matter how hard she's begged or cajoled."

What Clarice did, well – NO! STOP NOW! But the carousel has its own painted ponies and greased-lightning motor and his painted pony rides on. What she did to the Dreamer was . . . well . . . wrong. He thought it was . . . extreme, but Clarice was always a high-strung woman, a nervous woman, and left so young without a mother when she-was-only-six and then her father slumped over the funnies when she was just nineteen, her lipstick leaving a red fluted stain on his bald pate, and, truly, she was at her wit's end over Maggie.

To his endless embarrassment and shame that last bad year, Clarice phoned him at the office one day and demanded he come home.

The Dreamer had let a boy touch her, Clarice had hissed angrily over the coils of telephone wire, the hidden underground cables, cables he himself had drawn, then, lowering her voice to a tortured whisper, *You know, Down-there.*

No, he did not know, and he did not want to know and God knows he did not want to come home. But he did come. And what Clarice did, well, it was, well . . . wrong, just wrong. He had always thought that.

Then the poison was swallowed.

They sent away for brochures to an expensive private girls' boarding school. Beautiful grounds, tall, picturesque leafy trees and attractive buildings, carefully kept flower beds, a dining hall with crystal water glasses and white linen tablecloths and silverware that gleamed. They thought the Dreamer might like a private school better than the local high school, which she loathed. She'd be better able to cope with school then and, therefore, didn't it follow, with her life?

She sat hunched over in her quilted pink housecoat on her bed, the elbow-length sleeves not quite covering up all the slices and cigarette burns. She barely glanced at the brochures.

"Horseback riding, needlepoint, etiquette classes, cooking classes," Clarice gushed. But Maggie did not so much as raise her lowered eyelids to Clarice's or his face. It was as if invisible weights held them lowered, so lowered and still, they lay, white lashes against her cheeks like crescent moons. In the end she consented to raise those weighted eyelids but looked at only one photograph in the entire brochure.

"See how attractive the rooms are?" Clarice enthused.

The Dreamer looked away from the brochure and lay down on her bed and stared up into the ceiling. Finding blue-cloaked demons there?

They knew they had lost.

They even agreed to send her to a psychiatrist. The psychiatrist said that they must send her away. Well, it was a shock. Send their own away? To one of those places? A Crazy House like where he had been? But of course the Dreamer did not know that he had ever been in a Crazy House. Not then. No one in the family knew except his wife. Not yet. Not then.

The psychiatrist said, "Her arms, her legs, self-mutilation, the poison . . . very serious. . . ." On and on. . . . He said she should be committed to a sanatorium out in the countryside and he knew of a very fine one with a good reputation, a very old, well-known sanatorium. Top-notch, he said, allowing a small wink as he made a circle of his thumb and forefinger; the wink, the circle fashioned of forefinger and thumb, his word, his bond.

In the end, they gave up, gave in, and sent her away like the doctor said they should, all the proper papers signed. But he'd never trusted a psychiatrist yet. Not in all these years.

Clarice told him, "Those damn psychiatrists. You know they blame everything on us. The parents. That's the way those Freudians or whatever they are do it. That's how they think. I read that in one of my magazines. What did we ever do but love her?"

He raised one finger to his lips. "*Shh, she'll hear you,*" he whispered fiercely. He realized suddenly that everyone, the whole family, had been whispering between the walls of the Glass House for months. As if someone were dying – or had already died. The Dreamer, the ghost in her long white nightgown moving dreamlike, like one hypnotized, through the attic rooms clutching her jazz albums and slender volumes of Sylvia Plath tightly to her, Gertrude Stein glaring out of the wall.

Clarice had always tended to talk in a loud voice even when in a mellow mood, and when angry her voice and words echoed and tumbled through every room in the House that Timothy built. She had momentarily forgotten that they no longer spoke out loud in the Glass House but spoke only in whispers.

The great blind worms lie in tight-coiled white balls, like fists.

Timothy weeps and the carousel grinds slowly to a halt, the motor sparking-blue flint. The painted red and gold and blue snorting pony is still. Timothy weeps because he knows she is more like him than any of his other children. Sensitive, afraid, fists always raised and held up expecting the next blow, readying herself for it. She was born with those little ways of hers — the singing-speaking, the rhyming every word together, that fascination with spinning things, coils of wire, lengths of rope, hour after hour watching leaves fall one by one, hundreds of them falling from the autumn trees, entranced by blades of grass, lying on her stomach and gazing into them.

Counting them?

Seeing what?

Green demons?

It baffled and frightened him and made him afraid for her, more afraid than for anyone else in his family. His heart felt bruised and tender. In the end he felt angry at her for being born odd.

For being weak like him.

Rightness and order. Was it too much to ask with Ian Glass dead on Gibraltar in '42? The Rock a skeleton in the harsh sunlight, Ian's bones gleaming white as the jagged white bones of the Rock and his friends drowning and the cats and the dogs gone beneath the water's surface (deep, deep eyes looking at masters, begging please please) without a trace, and the vivid-painted parrots screaming, the monkeys howling and weeping, poor Reggie's tiny soft clutching hands, and him seeing the brains of other Fly Boys, friends all, splatter and burn, dangling straps of their Fly Boys' caps burning, and wound like hangman's nooses around their broken necks.

When the white doves fly over the blue cliffs of Dover . . .
When would the War . . .
Would it ever . . .
Be over . . . ?
End . . . ?
Beautiful Dreamer, wake unto me. . . .
When will you wake?
Will the War ever end?
When the white doves fly over the blue cliffs of Dover . . .
Beautiful Dreamer, dreaming wake . . . will you?
Ever . . . ?

He longs for the bats' wings to engulf his face, for their minute humanlike hands, their minute humanlike fingers, to gouge wounds into his flesh like the red bleeding trails left by skating razor blades.

The whale's eye is turned to him, a flat black stone. The yellow eyes of the falcon, the hunter, follow him in his dreams. The red eyes of the bats dart to his face in questions. The wolf howls eerie into a black night. It is all a dream. He remembers the bats, their wings spread out and laid over his body in a mourning cape. The cats drowned. The dogs drowned. The monkeys. The parrots went mad. His friends died a-howling in the death-silence. The sea dense as crushed black velvet. And not an answer to be found there in the killing sea to all the death and madness, the plane smouldering, smoking, sinking, the sea smooth, flat and ungiving as a plate.

He remembers Clocks at the Hospital, a patient there who had been on the Pacific front and a prisoner in a Japanese POW camp. Clocks wore clocks all over his body. Each clock was set to a different time. The clock dangling from his right wrist was set to 4:30 a.m., which was when the prisoners rose and received their bowl of rice with maggots swimming in it and sometimes water in a rusty metal cup and not always water.

The clock dangling from his left wrist was set to 6:00 a.m., when one was often kicked repeatedly and had a bamboo rod laid across one's back.

He wore a clock on each ankle. One clock was set to 4:00 p.m., the other to 5:00 a.m., the two worst beatings he ever received clocked in.

Another clock strapped above his elbow was set to

10:00 a.m. – a time of a desultory card-playing, stealing cigarettes, catching rats to eat, rolling tobacco for smokes, scraping each precious shred of tobacco from off the dirt floor.

And then there was The Clock, a solid-gold watch fob that had been his father's that sat taped square in the centre of Clocks' forehead that was set to 2:00 p.m. This, Clocks explained, was the time, near as he could recall, that he had been put in the sweat box and carried around the prison yard by other prisoners for three hours. "Ironic, ain't it?" Clocks always added with a faint smile. "I was in the box two times. Two times drowned and died in my own stinking, filthy sweat," Timothy remembers Clocks saying through tears, sometimes screaming through tears.

Timothy remembers how sometimes he and other patients would sing, chant, "Oh I'm surely going to Heaven 'cause I've spent my time in Hell," Clocks leading the sing-along with the waving of the clock dangling from his right wrist, the clocks at his ankles clanking as he kept time with his feet.

Timothy remembers another man who had nightmares every night. Always the same nightmare. About being burned alive in an iron box. He had been one of the first Allies to enter Auschwitz, opening it up at the end of the War, where often twelve thousand people were killed in a single day. And he swore he'd seen at least twelve thousand corpses thrice over.

"These were people, God man, these were people, human beings!" he said to Timothy once and then fainted dead away in Timothy's arms. He'd seen the ovens, the charred human bones and emptied eye sockets, and the walking, breathing skeletons that were once named human.

Timothy learned from the War and the people he knew then that in war, as in poetry and novels, people are seen as raw material. The whale, the falcon, the bats' questioning eyes, the wolf's eerie howl are all asking of him, *And who-o are you-u?*

Timothy answers, *I am all these things, all these memories and more. I am the man locked into nightmares. I am the man in the opium dream.*

He dreams and rocks with it. He dreams of the Fly Boys. Another sandstorm has come up, the big red one, the worst. They are drowning in it and trying to climb out of it. Trying to climb up a wall of gritty blood. There are hundreds of Fly Boys climbing, climbing the walls of red sand, the walls of blood. They climb on ladders, ladders strung across the great rising red walls of sand. The ladders are made of broken glass, murderous glass beads. Their hands bleed. Their feet bleed. They slip and slide in the wall of their own red blood. They do not look human, more like hundreds of crawling bugs, bugs with eyes that bulge out with the nightmares held behind them.

The glass ladders sway. The Fly Boys bleed. Gain a few inches, then slip down again, hands torn open and red, skin peeled back and laid open so that there is only raw flesh and white bone left exposed. When the glass ladders sway they make a tinkly, dreamy sound, like wind chimes. The sun is hot-white so that the Fly Boy-Bugs are black shadows scurrying, weeping, howling along with the howling wind of the red sandstorm.

Timothy struggles to a surface, some surface in this subterranean world in the Place of Not. He is groggy, he is sweating, he is Not-Dead, Not-Alive, Born-Not, and he realizes that the Fly Boys in the dream like him aren't going to die just yet, not for a while, maybe a long while, for this dream he realizes is a dream of the Inferno itself. *All Ye who enter here, abandon hope....*

But it is that little, little hope that damn near kills you, fragile and intricate as a spider's web and as easily broken.

He remembers running in terror after hope through the streets of London, his spider monkey Reginald's tiny grey hands clinging to his neck and Reginald chattering wildly, insanely, weeping great monkey tears, the walking, screaming fire-sticks all around them. He had been on leave in London and staying in a friend's flat, Reginald and he both asleep in the big bed with a down-filled mattress and freshly laundered white sheets. And then there was a sound, a great shattering thunder, and Timothy startled awake and saw in horror the red fire-tears sliding oily down through the black night sky.

In one moment, less, Timothy picked up the little monkey and sailed out the door and over the dark gaping space where once the stairway landing had been, and he did not stop running. He ran down the stairs, those that were left, and flew over the ones that were not and out into the street. The sky was alive with the sliding red and orange fire-tears, hot and slick as oil, and howling in the streets were moving sticks of fire.

In his shock, it took Timothy a few seconds to realize that these walking sticks of fire were people, their howls scarcely human, as he ran with Reginald, ran after hope through the blazing streets under the smoke-filled sky. Hope was the Underground. They would be safe in the tunnels there. Running, running. He did not know if he was screaming as Reginald was screaming. It did not matter. The whole night was alive with screams and howls from ground to sky. Heaven had split open, bleeding fire.

He did not know how long he ran or even if he was aware that he was running, aware only of having to catch that little hope that lay just up ahead, around the next corner, or the next. He saw one fire-stick topple over, crack right in two at the middle, charred and blackened.

That night he caught hope. Once they were in the tunnels with the hundreds of others huddled there with vacant eyes or mad eyes, the sensible eyes saying, "Let's get it over and done with and then make some tea," he tried to calm Reginald.

"Look, little pal," he said to the tiny grey monkey, "you've still got your red bandanna. What a brave good boy, and with your wonderful red bandanna too!" Reginald crawled into his arms and buried his little grey head in Timothy's armpit and clung there against him.

And the great white worms, on sensing Timothy's dreaming, blink, something touching their blindness for a brief moment other than their own dim pulsing.

19.

NEURONS ARE EYE-SHAPED. I told The Kid this one afternoon just before he went out bike riding. Interestingly so, don't you think? They are white and eye-shaped. Yeah, The Kid agreed, that is interesting. Gotta go now and meet the Boys, he said, grabbing a bottle of Gatorade from the refrigerator and planting a kiss on my cheek. Shoulder-length curls flew out behind him like dark-golden wind as he raced out the door.

If he could have stayed longer I would have told him that each neuron has tiny stemlike membranes spreading from it like thin threads linking one neuron to the next, transmitting along the information, the knowledge, linking it all up. Some neurons have only a few stemlike membranes, one or two, others more, four, five, five like a starfish.

Neurons like starfish, or four tiny stems reaching out like the points of a star, stars in the dark night of the Alzheimer's patient's brain. Neurons and God. Neurons are eye-shaped and is it accidental that the nerves of the brain that hold all information and knowledge are like windows looking inwards? Eyes turned in. You could look on the brain as an old radio receiver and the spirit as the electromagnetic waves travelling through it with all the information, all the knowledge a person gleans in a lifetime. It almost makes one believe in God. I have always believed evolution and God can co-exist quite sweetly together.

I've had arguments in bars over that one, one man slamming his beer glass against the tabletop so violently that the glass shattered and beer spread in white foam and amber liquid across the table and onto the floor. But, listen, he'd never had fire rip through his brain and I have. That too nearly makes one believe in God. Fire flowing through the brain and yet you live.

I sit here late into the night, the cigarettes smouldering in the ashtray, the fierce Dragon-Birds winking smoke from their cruel eyes, the coffee in the pot grows cold. Stockings sits on my desk nuzzling my cheek with his furry damp cheek as I pound away at my keyboard. When Stockings loves you he drools on you, which isn't so far from human behaviour at all when it comes to love. The clock hand moves relentlessly towards the no man's land of night, where every step you take you take Alone and in the Dark. I've gone through ancient creaking photograph album after ancient creaking photograph album until my eyeballs ache and glaze over with a protective sheen like ice.

I have thought and thought long and hard about all of this. About the Glass Family and the truth of it, which I feel with a certainty is Timothy Glass. What I don't know is all the whys of who he is. It may be that these long notes I make night after night will only be hidden away on some high closet shelf and taken out by me on cold winter nights to be read under the covers by flashlight. And yet . . . and yet . . . I know if I write the truest that I can, write not one Real-Not word, it won't just sit high atop a closet shelf.

My journey with T. Glass began nearly forty-three years ago. And continues still.

Could it be that I could forgive?

Even – something more?

I think of his brain and weep over all those loose tubes in his radio receiver; first one tube loosened and then the static began, then another tube and another and another, static-staticstatic, hot-white fuzz for a brain, and when his whole radio receiver breaks down it will be like death. Oh I know The Sisters Three and just about everyone else thinks that the old receiver is busted up completely now, that he drifts in a coma, but me, I'm not so sure. The auras say, *He is in there somewhere and he is alive and he knows*.

His journey, I think, like mine, is not yet over. I think now he must be travelling back and back and back, hodge-podge in this travelling back, the memories as he travels far into the past leaping up here and there randomly.

And his face. I can see it in his face, the backwards travelling. His face goes back and back, as if in his Alzheimer's he is searching for or becoming his original face. The Beginning Face. My first memory of a change in his face was of coming off the elevator that winter afternoon and seeing his mouth. It had changed shape. Pursed. Next I think his cheekbones blurred somehow. His blue eyes paled. His whole face grew tighter, closed-in, smaller.

◡

I fan the photographs out in an ever-widening circle like a deck of truth-cards, like the trembling of tarot cards held in a shaking hand, fanned out in a circle, the circular face of a clock, the minutes steadily falling like rain, like tears, like bombs.

Here, on the bright-purple and indigo-blue and gold Jazz Festival calendar taped to the wall above my desk. 1991. Time has by-passed George Orwell's fateful 1984, steadily, inexorably moving on, Time marching, Time a-running, Time speeding like a silver-bullet train raising glinting sparks from the iron tracks, and yet in these photographs all remains as it was, untouched by Time, frozen, suspended, unchanging.

Timeless as the whirring of blue dragonfly wings over yellow grasses, and the hallucinatory wispy pale-grey clouds of tiny insects hovering over a summer field of purple wildflowers on a hot August day, shimmering like sheets of cellophane.

Shimmering like mirages, like madness.

Here, halfway round the clock face, is a faded photograph worn almost white with sepia brown spreading through it like a stain. It is a photograph of my father at five years of age with his unsmiling father standing by the side of their summer house up at the lake, the name of the lake long ago lost in my father's unravelling mind, the green grass bleached to white snow in the faded photograph.

Another photograph, quarter-point on the clock face, is of Timothy Glass, seven years old, leaning against a tree at the farm, cap in one hand, a giant white puffball, found out by the marsh past the haying field, his prize, secured under his other hand and arm. Nothing has changed. There he is: Timothy Glass forever seven, forever holding his boy's cap in one hand.

There is one of Timothy Glass and Clarice on their wedding day, standing outside the big heavy wooden double doors of the church they were married in out in British Columbia. Timothy, impossibly young, wears his Air Force uniform, a dark tie tightly, expertly knotted at his neck, his starched white shirt collar glimpsed above the dark lapels of his uniform, the Fly Boy cap held in the crook of his arm, his hand reaching to Clarice's hand, into it, his fingers wound through hers. Clarice is wearing a modest suit-dress, the skirt hangs loosely and just grazes her shapely knees. Three big round buttons are on the form-fitting jacket, a splendid white corsage nestles on the collar, pinned above her left breast. She wears silk stockings and shiny pumps and a hat with a little veil and feather – the little green hat? Her hair is long and curly and, gleaming, rides in dark clouds on her shoulders.

A photograph of Timothy Glass in the RCAF looking like a matinée idol, so lean and handsome with a trim moustache above his well-shaped, slender upper lip. His eyes stare with an intensity, a darkness, unwaveringly into the camera's lens, his hair is slicked down flat against his skull, a part sharp and straight as an arrow lies just over the place where the ragged eyebrow was birthed so long ago.

There is an album whose red wooden covers have nearly fallen completely apart and off and are held loosely, barely together, by black laces. In my father's hand, written across the cover in black ink, the title:

THE LIFE AND TIMES OF THE GLASS FAMILY
– 1948 TO 1951 –
(When 3 + 1 = 4)
Maggie Laura Glass born June 8th, 1948

There is one photograph of me among the scattered photographs falling from the scarcely held-together album that seems to me to be exactly me. It is how I have always and will forever see myself through that long tunnel of mind's eye. Undimmed by Time.

In the small black-and-white photograph I am three years old in a frilly little sundress, hair white as dust. Coming into the frame is a finger without a person attached to it. Only part of a forearm can be seen pointing out just past me, giving me some kind of order, some sort of instruction to follow, and my big eyes look confused, anxious, but at the same time defiant, my white brows are furrowed tightly in concentration, for I always had to concentrate very hard on whatever was said to me; and I think furrowed too with consternation, mouth corners turned a little downwards, my mouth a little open – as if to speak? Protest?

I am her still, forever frozen at three, white hair like clouds, like dust, big wide eyes worried, filled with that terrible unending anxiety, always struggling to comprehend what the rest of the world seems to take with ease in calm stride but always, always the defiance in that worried face peers out past all else that dwells there. I remember constantly saying in my mind in tormented whispers to the Glass Family, to the teachers, and to the guidance counsellors and to the schoolmates, JUST LEAVE ME ALONE!

And later in high school I earned the nickname, which was bandied about the school corridors, of the girl with the Don't-Fuck-With-Me Face. Had I, in my Greenwich Village black uniform, actually looked so fierce, so ferocious? When all the while I thought I was slinking through the halls with my slender volumes of Sylvia Plath and the fat books of Richard Wright – especially *Native Son* with its character Bigger Thomas – looking exactly what I was: terrified.

Once, I suspect, I loved all my family but somewhere a separation, a cleaving, came. Some of the cleaving I can still see as clearly as the ticking clock hand falling in knife strokes on the clock face before me on my desk.

My first consciousness, awareness of a cleaving, of an Otherness, came early. I knew clearly even before two years of age that I was born with a secret beat, with rhythms and secret songs spinning in the dust motes and sunlight and shadows in the gardens and attic rooms. And, later, that in this secret beat, this music, were stories and poems, a continual rhythmic story-song locked in the Me that no one else could see. And, most certainly of all, I knew they could not hear it.

Even before I was capable of speech I knew they could not hear what I heard, the music blazing through the attic windows, the thrumming beat in my rocking body in the crib, the secret, ceaseless rhythms beating my head against the crib bars the walls the chairs the floors in my hiding song.

I knew this, for I would tell my family my version of things. And always, inevitably, they'd say, "No, no, that isn't true. That isn't so. This is the way it really is." Every truth I ever gave them they called lie. I learned early on to make what I called "translations." I would give my family the answer they wanted and expected of me, and, in the same moment I answered them aloud, within my hiding, mute self, I'd give my own *real* answer.

Once, I said to my psychiatrist, who is kind, a friend, and all mine, "Even my goddamn dog died!" And I laughed. He smiled and asked me about my dog, his eyes intent upon my face.

The goddamn dog did die. When I was four years old my parents bought me a beautiful little collie pup because I had no playmates. They thought he would be a good companion for me. He was beautiful, all gold and white and soft brown like sunlight and rich toffee, and I loved him with every fragment of a heart that had somewhere, somehow stopped loving almost everything and everyone. I named him My-Boy. My-Boy lived to the ripe old age of four months.

One winter morning Lillian and Dinah (who were only two years old and therefore cannot be blamed) let my puppy outside. No one else in the house was up yet. No one but the twins knew My-Boy was running free outside. The house slept, all but Lillian and Dinah. My golden collie boy ran and ran.

Later when he was discovered missing, Daddy took the car out and went searching for him, patrolling all the streets of the neighbourhood near and far while I prayed beside my bed, weeping, weeping and promising God anything, anything at all if he'd just bring My-Boy home to me. My-Boy who loved me. My father returned hours later and said he'd looked and looked but could find My-Boy nowhere.

The clock hand falls like a meat cleaver. I was inconsolable with grief. But not just for months, for years.

Every time I walked the roads to school or wandered in the golden fields or deep shadowed ravines I called out for My-Boy. Every time I saw a stray collie dog I thought he was My-Boy and would weep and beg and try to drag the poor confused dog home with me. But, of course, none of these gold and white and toffee collie boys was My-Boy.

My-Boy was much closer to home than I ever knew. He was buried under the dirt floor in our garage. Daddy had found him that first day. He'd found My-Boy by the side of Kingston Road, which was just below Fairfield Boulevard. He'd been hit by a car and was bloody and broken and dead. Daddy gently scooped up My-Boy in his arms and brought him home to the garage, where he dug a small My-Boy grave (for My-Boy was very small) and buried him.

It wasn't until years later when I was nine and was given a new collie pup that I found out that My-Boy had been dead all those five long years. My parents had agreed between them that it was best for me to think of My-Boy as alive but just still and always missing.

A later cleaving remembered: Rachel, Lillian and Dinah, Daddy and Clarice, and I are all having Sunday dinner. Me and The Sisters Three are all grown-up. We all have children and The Sisters Three have husbands. The Kid is sitting beside me, happily eating roast beef rich with gravy and purple beets with melted butter and golden roast potatoes, tiny green peas. My sisters are eating with their husbands and children. Rachel leans across the sparkling sterling silverware and crystal wine glasses, over the white damask tablecloth, and says to me, "Do you remember how you broke your leg when you were five, Maggie?"

"Sure. I was standing on the hassock on one foot pretending to be a bird, a whooping crane maybe. Or a flamingo. Something like that."

"No," Rachel said. "No, that's not what happened. I pushed you!" A wide smile leaped wild across Rachel's face and Clarice's voice came shrieking over the prettily laid Sunday dining table, "YOU DID NOT!"

But I have an earlier memory. I am five and my leg is newly broken and in a heavy cast from toes to hip, stuck out straight in front of me like a big fat white ruler on the wine-coloured hassock. I am sitting in the pale-green chair in the living room with my metal TV tray, eating Kraft Dinner with ketchup, strips of bacon, and slices of bread with butter and watching "Superman" on the television set.

A little behind and to the left of me is the kitchen door off the dining room, and it is open and I can hear all the Glass Family in there laughing and talking, forks clinking against plates. Laughter, loud voices. I turn my head in the direction of the open kitchen door. I can see the egg-yolk-yellow walls and I can hear all the sounds of the Glass Family; their talk and their laughter and their clinking forks against their plates and my eyes fill with sudden hot tears. When a truth hits you full force even if you've always known it, if only in a shadow-way, it can make your eyes spring alive hot and wet.

I remember this clearly as yesterday's sunrise. It was winter. Beyond the big living-room window was a black night, ridges of cold frozen-white snow, and icicles hanging in daggers from the eaves. I knew then in that moment that this was how it had always been and always would be with the Glass Family and me. The Glass Family all sitting down together eating and talking and laughing, without me. I was Outside.

They were Inside, where the sun shone warm and egg-yolk yellow from their walls and they were all talking together, hand joining hand, making a brittle ribbon, a glittering glass necklace: the Glass Family.

Without me. And oblivious to that fact, almost completely.

After all, didn't they have to be?

To Be.

I remember how Superman in his cape with the big S insignia on it whipping out behind him in the wind as he flew and ran faster than a locomotive and leaped tall buildings in a single bound blurred in front of my eyes and I turned and looked out at the black winter night and saw my reflection in the windowpane, thin and pale white, drawn, grown even thinner and paler since the break in my leg, tears like silver snail tracks running down my face.

And the truth of how real my insight at five was was that nearly twenty-five years later when Rachel told me she had pushed me, something I had no memory of, I did not so much as flinch or blink with surprise. I felt, in fact, nothing, nothing at all, and went calmly back to eating my splendidly prepared Sunday dinner with the Glass Family. Had I really, after all, ever expected it to be otherwise, even in my not-knowing? My buried memories, in that stinking bog where memories, secrets even unto ourselves, smoulder like War gasses, like fog.

How many more secrets, how many more cleavings in tender, falling knife strokes up to that hot summer nightmare afternoon when Clarice buried me in bloodied Kotex?

Never, never tell the truth about the Glass Family, Maggie, or you'll be sorry as sorry, sorry as you can be, sorry as sorry. . . .

What is there left to lose?

Any more.

Clarice hissing out, *A boy . . . Down-there.*

My father's arm, the bolt the door.

A sky turned black.

Screams.

Mine.

Secrets. How many more secrets, how many more tender, mercy-giving strokes of the knife blade until . . . until . . . one is emptied?

Emptied of everything.

My second collie, a beautiful female named My-Girl, with her pedigree's elegant, narrow snout, was grey and white and black so that she appeared a ghostly blue, like an eerie wolf in the distance in daylight, a magical night creature in moonlight. My-Girl developed epilepsy when I was thirteen years old and was, as the euphemism so nicely words it, "put to sleep."

Or a more apt euphemism perhaps – put down.

Ironic, no?

Epilepsy bleeding into epilepsy, two beloved collie dogs, both my dear and best and only friends and both dead before their lives had been lived to maturity, finished out. Some Island people believe that unfinished lives, in dying, are the ghosts who wander the Earth, forever restless, forever searching for that which was robbed them, forever unfinished. I hear both my collie dogs, My-Boy and My-Girl, howling still, pawing at my door with blunted claws and bloody paws to be let in and given a warm corner to curl up in, a kiss, arms wrapped around wonderful, warm furry necks and given a gentle stroking hand.

Watch out.

Insanity, along with sparking wires, electrical shorts, smouldering, smoking blue fuses, and white licking flame, may be catching.

Even the goddamn dog dies.

20.

SPRING HAS EDGED into early summer, an early summer hot and green-bursting. Flowers bloom forth hot-pink and bleeding into reds and purples, verdant green sprouting everywhere. Sprinklers are already turned on, despite the earliness of the season, doing their hypnotic fan dances across burning green, carefully sculpted lawns. The sky is a violent slash of blue on the day my friend drives me to the hospital to see Daddy. It has been a long time, six weeks, since I've been able to bring myself to visit him.

My friend is a new friend, or very nearly new. He is a special friend. He is my next-door neighbour. I met him when I went to his door to borrow Band-aids for my bleeding fingertips. I'd been pounding away at the keyboard for so long, a little over thirty-six hours, that blood began to flow under my fingernails. He smiled at me when I showed him my bloody nails and I thought, Smile at me again.

Just as nice as the fact that he is a very special friend is that The Kid likes him.

I try ineptly in word sketches to tell him who my father was before the Alzheimer's settled in grey cobwebs over his brain, cloaking it, before the coma drifted him into unknown primeval seas, between dangerous high cliffs.

"Daddy could pinpoint any battle in any century, the generals, and the given year or years of all the battles in history. From Attila the Hun to Ghengis Khan. Why, he could draw you a map of the Mongolian Empire," I tell him.

"He could have a very good wit. Some people thought him taciturn, but he really could be very charming and funny."

My friend's large long-fingered hands twist the blue steering wheel to the left.

I tell him, "I remember one favourite story of Daddy's that he told us over and over when we were all kids at the dinner table about when he was a little boy attending his family's church. The minister was giving a fire and brimstone sermon as usual and there was a woman there who had this little baby with her and the baby began to cry. And cry. And cry. The baby would just not stop crying. Loud, shrieking cries.

"And this minister in his white and gold Anglican robes always got worked up with his fiery sermons but, what with the intensity and passion of his sermon and the loudly wailing baby and his own fist pounding the pulpit at a shattering rate, the good minister's nose began to bleed and bleed. Profusely.

"Still, he went on with his sermon and still the baby wailed loudly, louder, louder, until finally the minister flung out one white-robed arm dramatically, blood sailing from his nostrils in twin red streams down his white-robed sleeves, splattering the pulpit and the Bible laid open on it, and he screamed, 'Get that goddamn baby out of my goddamn church!'"

My friend smiles. He has a silver-grey lion's mane of hair like my father has a snow-white lion's mane of hair, and he is built like a linebacker and is as tall as a strong tree. Nearly. Six foot five and a bit. We are getting near the hospital zone.

"He's extremely intelligent," I tell my friend.

My friend's name is Peter.

"Or maybe now with the coma? Maybe not so bright now, not any more."

My friend says something that tumbles me over with the force of its echoes. He says, "Your father may be lying in a coma, but somewhere he knows. He's still alive and he knows."

This is fated.

This is kismet.

I want to marry him.

I will marry him.

Recently, over cold beers in a rundown tavern in our neighbourhood with pool tables adorned in torn green felt and plastic gold-and-blue Tiffany lamps hanging from the low, smoky ceiling and the juke box blaring, I told Peter about the Night of the Knife, of Shadow's breath hot on my face, Shadow's fingers hard on my throat, his wet lips hot on my ear, The Kid asleep in the bed beside me, tender, innocent cherry-red cherub lips breathing in-out. I told him about phoning my father at three a.m. and of my father's betrayal.

Well, what do you expect me to do about it?

And of my mother's angry hiss of hatred the next night when The Kid and I slept at my parents' house, the lamp switched off twenty times for each of the twenty times I switched it on. How she hated me that night, I told him.

Peter narrowed his sky-blue eyes and lit up a Rothmans cigarette and signalled the waitress in her short, shiny green miniskirt and gold blouse for two more bottles of beer.

I had told Peter about my many months of poring over the photograph albums since the onset of my father's illness and of trying to come to terms with him, of his experiences in the War and the opium he smoked in the desert with the other Fly Boys after their Arab hosts and local traders had led them to its pleasures, the nightmares, the haunting worlds of opium dreams.

The waitress brought the cold bottles of beer. I lit up a Du Maurier. Peter squinted, eyes narrowed to the red tip of his cigarette.

A long pause.

"Then –"

"Maybe he was tired of fighting. All the wars."

"What the hell! You think I wasn't – am not – tired of fighting wars too? All my wars?"

"Sure you were and are. But remember, he was about the same age as The Kid and dropping bombs from the coffin – that's what it was called, you said, right? – the coffin of the plane. Nineteen years old."

I smiled. It was the truth. The Kid lying on my belly still attached to me by the umbilical cord, the last time we'd ever be so joined, his dark, slightly almond-shaped eyes staring up into mine as if he'd always known me and expected me to be there, saying, "Hi, hi, I'm your kid!"

I knighted him with a little bit of birth blood drawn across his dark-gold eyebrows.

To keep him Special and Safe.

Always.

The knighthood. The Kid. Sir Bug. Honey. Never his birth name, the one written on the birth certificate. Reuben Glass, Winter, 1972. Safe and Special. Always. My love. My mother-love.

"I've been thinking about your mother ever since you told me what she did," Peter said. "I remember what you told me about what happened that afternoon. She doesn't sound like a mother to me. Not any mother I've ever known."

"But she is. Was. She was my mother."

Peter knows about wars and mothers. He is older than I am. He was a baby in Europe when the War broke out. He remembers that when the bombs fell and there were blackouts his parents would wheel him helpless in his crib, the crib churning on rickety wheels pell-mell down through all the passageways of the house to the basement, where he would be safer. He remembers the racing crib, the terrifying speed of it, his tight tiny fists, his heart clenched and bursting out of his small breast. He remembers his mother's frantic whispers, his father's hushed, rushing voice – him and the two grown-ups, all he had to trust in the world, alone, in the dark while the bombs screamed and thundered about them and the black rain fell and fell.

He knows about mothers and mother-love. His mother ran with him in her arms across Europe and eventually escaped to Sweden, where they joined his father who had gone on ahead. In the end, mother and child, they made it to Sweden, to husband and father.

"That is why my teeth were so bad. Got soft. No healthy foods. My baby teeth," Peter once remarked, "were compared to a mouth full of porridge by the first dentist I saw in Sweden."

He dimly remembers a dark night, water lapping against a boat, moonlight a white, thin-fingered bone lying across the black water, soldiers boots heavy above them, above their heads, guns, his mother clutching him, her hand clamped over his mouth so that the soldiers would not hear him crying. The soldiers found them in their hiding place anyway, his mother weeping, humiliation, defeat. The heavy boots taking them off the boat herded mother and infant back to shore and danger. The War, the War, the War, it was everything when Peter was a child.

He has her memory of American planes strafing her as she ran with him in her arms down a rutted road, to hide behind trees, to dodge the bullets.

That night I spoke to Peter about mother-love, my knowledge of it. I drew hard and long on my cigarette.

We talked again about that hot steamy summer afternoon when I was fifteen. Rachel watching with a curious, detached interest, but not surprised at all. No, not that. It was almost . . . almost as if she knew, as if she'd expected

Clarice to do something like this one day. To one of us. One of the girls. Most probably to me, The It in the Glass Family. Surprised-Not that Clarice had done it, and not surprised that the one she did it to was me. An unspoken conspiracy, the choosing of The It.

"What could anyone have done?"

"Mother-love? Heh . . . I've thought. About that. I've considered the hard-fact that my mother had no mother as an example to emulate. No one, no one at all to teach her how to be a mother. Maybe she loved me once but I think that that love – the mother-love – stopped a long time back. Probably so far back, so long ago, that I cannot recall it, pinpoint it, the cessation of it – not in my conscious mind.

"In dreams maybe. In dreams I recall it. The ending of it all. In dreams I have a sharp awareness of its end. Freud would have fun! What fun! Sometimes in my dreams she buries me in shit. It seeps up past my mouth-hole, travels right into my mouth-hole halfway down the child-throat and into my nose-holes and up to the rims, the very edges of my eyes, the rims of my eyes brimming with shit . . . my eyelashes not white any more. But once – maybe – mother-love I had once. . . ."

"Your father?" Peter said. "What does your psychiatrist say about him? His love? Your father? Did he – ? What does he think?"

A loud blast from the juke box drowned out my answer. I mouthed words in the dark amidst crashing thunder, only whispers unheard buried in a storm.

"What?" Peter asked, leaning forward.

"He says he thinks that my father loved me. Yes, he said that. That, out of all my family, he loved me. My father. And he thinks my father knows – that I love him."

Peter's mouth moved into a scowl, whether at my doctor's pronouncement of the father-love for me, or at thoughts of my own mother-love, or at his own memories, I do not know. He rose from the round table we sat at and went over to a pool table and hoisted a pool cue in his hands. Coloured balls were racked up, spinning, clattering, ricocheting across the green felt. He played someone who had a big beer gut and whose hairy, pale fleshy belly could be seen through an opening in his shirt where two buttons were either missing or undone.

A cigarette dangled from Peter's mouth corner, the smoke sailed blue in streamers around his face, making wreaths like blue haloes around his head, but it did not seem to bother him. He never once, the whole time he played, removed the cigarette from his mouth. Time ticked by and the coloured balls rolled and clattered and the cigarette remained stuck to that one mouth corner, the butt growing smaller and smaller, disappearing, the red-embered tip of the cigarette drawing ever closer to his lips.

Peter is a better-than-good pool player but does not play pool often any more. Hardly ever. He is – was – could still be, an excellent pool player. His friends and acquaintances all tell me that he was so good at it he could have made a living from his pool playing alone. I once asked him why he stopped playing for money and why he stopped playing pool almost entirely.

"My mind moved on, restless, relentless," he had said.

Peter speaks six or seven languages and reads calculus books for pleasure, rapidly turning the pages the way other people settle cosily into an armchair with a John Grisham or Danielle Steele novel.

Once he went all the way to Mexico to get away from language when he was fed up with people talking and talking but not speaking language, not real language. I said I understood that. Often I've sat in rooms with people and wanted to shout, to scream, "Say something, anything, that is real and true."

He's a two-fisted drinker but a born gentleman and doesn't swear freely. On our first date he carried me home in his arms from the restaurant the six blocks uphill to my front door.

On our third date he gave me his phone number, extending the bit of paper he wrote it on, saying, "I want you to have this." And then he kissed me goodnight for the first time.

What I've learned from this is that a two-fisted drinker ex-pool player born gentleman knows how to make love as adeptly, with as great and tender care as he reads calculus books and handles languages with fluency.

As I watched him bending over the pool table, just as the game was ending, Peter winning, I thought, Daddy would have loved him.

That truth brought sudden tears to my eyes, for I was as certain of it as I am of my own heartbeat, the throbbing in my pulse-place, the pain I am filled with, and knew too that my father, buried in the dark-shadowed rooms of his coma, would never know Peter; Peter, the only man I've ever loved. My father who thought I was not worthy. Of love. Beyond his own broken love for me.

I will marry him. He speaks six or seven languages. In the honours maths class at university they called him Spock, the professors and students alike. Already at that time a silver Latvian engagement ring (six silver triangular symbols with Latvian inscriptions on them marking the first meeting of lovers to the final knotting of that love, the consummation, the totality of it all) was hanging on a silver chain around my neck.

Peter sidled back to the table, the game over. "You mustn't be filled with hate. Not for him. Or for her," he said.

My Famous-Friend Doctor says that I am filled with pain, not hate, and that that pain and its ghosts are what make me write. And it is the writing that has kept me alive.

"Do you believe he is right?"

"Yes. The words. They were all I ever had. Until The Kid. They are my heartbeat, they are in the blood that The Kid flooded out on in a red tidal flow."

"What would you have done differently? Than your parents."

"You mean if I had had a kid like me? I'm not sure exactly. Back in the '50s seeing a psychiatrist was something that just wasn't done. Not by real, normal, regular people. Even in the early '60s it was still pretty taboo. Only the very rich or the insane saw psychiatrists in the 1950s and early '60s. I must have been ahead of my time because I remember when I was nine years old I wanted to be either a writer or an actress or a psychiatrist. Now my Famous-Friend

Doctor says, 'So you grew up and became a writer, and became all three.' So I guess everyone did not think psychiatry taboo, including my Famous-Friend Doctor, who is now in his mid-fifties. But I do know one thing."

"What?"

"I wouldn't have done what they all did to me, the Glass Family. I wouldn't have made my kid The It. Or done the rest of the things my mother . . ."

Yellow and black and white signs. HOSPITAL ZONE QUIET.

I want to grasp Peter's hand. Tightly hold it, hold him to me and say, Do you know me yet? Do you know me yet? But no one ever has. No one but The Kid and my Famous-Friend Doctor. I feel hopeless, given up, defeated. It moves through me like a sleepy cry.

"Underground parking," Peter says, annoyed.

We travel round and round in ever-decreasing circles, spiralling downwards past many white and black and yellow signs cautioning HOSPITAL ZONE QUIET. ADMITTING. EMERGENCY.

My mind wanders, travelling spaces. Tier after dark tier. Bluebeard's castle made of concrete and black tar and steel. Dark shadows. Stark white pools of light. Elevators. My mind floats, free-falling.

For some reason I am thinking of the Guys swimming in their oval glass bowl, The Kid's guppies, and their little black exclamation-point tails. I've always wondered where all the guppies went, the guppies disappearing, by ones and twos over the years. In the end there was only one, the Guy, big and fat, swimming round and round utterly and blissfully alone in the oval bowl with the little cut-glass tri-angle-like designs.

I am reminded for some reason of that long-ago early-spring day nearly fourteen years ago at Tim Horton's when The Kid and I had fled Toronto to Kitchener-Waterloo, the ice cracking in dirty brown skeins, wild brown grass pushing weakly, half-dead half-alive, struggling through the dirt-caked cracks in the sidewalk, the melting black pools of ice and the first fly of spring busily buzzing about the sugar bowls and the honeyed doughnuts.

I remember the exposed corpses of the birds, the sweet white safety and sanction of snow gone, the dogs sniffing at their entrails that lay uncoiled like gluey, sticky, scraggly black wires, sniffing at the dead birds with the glass-marbled bird eyes, and, later, the hunter-pussycat grinning around the rotting bird corpse he carried away between sharp, pointy teeth in his curved-up pink forever-smiling cat mouth.

The Guy, swollen and fat-black, had eaten all the other guppies, I realize that now. A cannibal. The Guy was a cannibal.

Funny, I never thought of it before. Not in all these years. It never occurred to me. Until now. Round and round. Peter cursing softly. Yellow parking-lot tickets etched with black squiggles legitimized with a tidy, perfectly round hole fashioned from a metal ticket puncher. Bureaucracy and organization are everything. Glassed-in booths. Men dressed in drab brown uniforms inside the glass booths. I think of Adolf Eichmann in the glass booth during the trial for his War crimes. There are underground elevators buried deep in the concrete and steel bowels of the parking lot. The elevator doors are painted yellow.

I remember once seeing on television a little boy of no more than four in Buchenwald holding a stick, probably using it for a toy as any child would. He was dressed in a little cap and a ragged jacket and short pants, black oversized shoes on his feet. He was trying to smile for the camera as children do and trying manfully not to cry, the camp an horrific still-life behind him. In the end his brave smile wavers, crumbles, collapses, and tears silver and large escape his huge dark eyes.

I thought when I looked into that little boy's face I was looking into the face of God.

But where was God? Not just that once but so many times?

I remember Peter telling me, "The Germans were kind to my mother and me. They gave us food."

I take some small hope from something I've gleaned from the writers I have read as we turn down yet another tier, deeper, deeper into the concrete and steel bowels of the parking lot. From the great writers, anyway. "In order to find your life you have to lose your life."

I have lost my life in many ways. I have only a Grade Nine education. The Shock Shop has made it hard to remember. For a long time, years, I could not write a word. For several years we had to live, The Kid and I, on ten dollars a week and we lived in awful slums. I've been beaten into epilepsy, raped, and abandoned by those that say they love you dearest and best, family.

Have I found my life? I am not sure. The Kid is part of

the finding, Peter too, my Famous-Friend Doctor, and alas, alas, my father. In that final falling of the knife blade flashing is one's life at last found? I don't know. I am no philosopher and think only of how my father will look now, withered and white, his eyelashes frost, his body a pale, bleached bone, his white lion's mane still thick and full and proud. I want only an Aspirin and a Clonazepam, a cigarette, a blue tab of Haldol, and out out out!

Where is God?

In the little boy in Buchenwald, in the huge silver tears spilling from his eyes down his face?

From God's eyes to his?

Peter told me that when he and his mother reached Sweden and his father, he was angry with his father.

"For abandoning us."

"But he didn't. He couldn't help it."

"I didn't know that then."

And once I told Peter's father, Sasha, that I was sure Peter was not really mad at him when they first met and his father laughed, a wide grin spread across his fine face, ear to ear, and he said emphatically, "No, he was mad! Mad! He was mad at me!" And Peter laughed and I laughed and we all laughed. His father and mother are wonderful people. To be able to laugh at such nightmares. Maybe that is when there is God, when you can laugh at such nightmares, maybe that is when the losing of your life is over and you find your life.

My headache has worsened. Will my father's hospital windowsills be banked with flowers in little plastic pots covered with glinting bright-green and blue foil with pretty cards tucked within the blooms? Will the television set be turned on with someone jumping up and down and kissing the handsome, gleaming-tooth-tooth host after just winning a brand-new washer and dryer *and* a brand-new car?

The hospital lights will shine whitely, brightly. In a hospital there is always twenty-four-hour daylight, courtesy of General Electric light bulbs. For if night were admitted, the possibility of death would enter those bright corridors.

Peter came to Canada when he was nine and he was still wearing wooden shoes, clogs, as children do in Sweden. One day he wore them to the local grocery store and three older boys started to make fun of his shoes. "Real nice shoes, kid. Real cool." Peter said yes, thank you, they were and they were very comfortable and functional too. The three followed him home, taunting him all the way. Peter went up the stairwell of the apartment he then lived in above a store with his parents and little sister. His sister was born in Sweden. The boys followed Peter.

Peter grabbed a hockey stick on the stairwell and beat them off with it.

I had to laugh when he told me that. Who were those bright Canadian-born-and-bred boys to think they could beat up and outlast a DP who'd run halfway across war-torn Europe and lived near a country where it is midnight for so many months that people kill themselves in huge numbers yearly.

At last we have found a parking space buried deep, deep in the concrete and steel and dark. "Better have a cigarette now before we go inside," Peter says. Yes, yes, I light up and we slide out of the car. My dress sticks to the backs of my legs with the heat. The elevators are dim yellow in the underground dark. I ask Peter if he has any Aspirin on him. He searches through his shirt pocket, his wallet. "No. I'll buy you a cold drink later and something to eat. Something cool to eat, melons, a salad."

The elevator doors slide open in the dimness. The elevators are like tombs. We move upwards out of the concrete bowels, out of Dante's circle of Hell, out of the bunkers. And all I can think of is that long-ago day looking out the window of Tim Horton's that morning we had just arrived in Kitchener-Waterloo, and wearily, weary beyond belief, closing my eyes and thinking, *The earth is a predator.*

Thinking, *In order to find your life you have to lose your life.*

And I have lost it many times, watching my father fade into shadow.

Courage.

Take.

I remember sometime after the Ballantine's scotch caper Daddy and I were out walking in a snowfall past the University of Toronto campus. "Stone 202 loud and singing and slurping," Daddy said indignantly.

I walked steadily on beside him, through the falling snow, my arm linked through his. The gentleman always, and walking on the outside, the elbow still proffered as soon as we were outside the door and on the sidewalk. The same gentlemanly nod of his head. Snow fell on my mittened hands, my eyelashes, my cheeks. I was thinking about it, trying to figure out the word puzzle. Then I saw it.

"The Staff, Daddy? Had the radio on loud, stone? 202? You mean Rock 102?" I knew the station. "And the boys with the mops drinking our scotch and dancing?"

"What I said," he muttered, his mouth all pulled in tight with drawn purse strings, like fingers pressing his lips in, drawing them tight together.

His arm no longer mellowed with warm scotch was not flesh and blood, his elbow crooked to me, my hand lay in it and it was glass, fine brittle glass, brittle as fine cracking crystal, his legs two stiff wires, his chin still tilted defiantly.

The elevator doors slide open into the Daylit world, the world where darkness and death are not permitted.

We walk down a sunny corridor to the elevator that will take us up to my father's floor.

Will the television set be on? Will shiny quarters be clattering gaily into the Coke machine in the hall? Will he have moved at all in the last week? Peter sees me close my eyes as we travel upwards to the seventh floor, Daddy's floor.

His fingers wrap over mine and he says, "Remember, he's still alive and he knows."

Courage.

I figure you don't run damn near starving halfway across Europe and are damn near killed more than once and twice and thrice for nothing.

21.

THE WINDOWSILLS ARE banked with fresh flowers. Silver, green, and blue glinting foil around the containers. Tasteful tiny gift-shop cards. Peter stands just inside the doorway of Daddy's room. Quarters clatter into the Coke machine out in the corridor but, thank God, the television set is not on.

The room is bright with sunlight. Daddy rides white on his white raft, metal bars raised. One of The Sisters Three, Dinah, is there. She is rearranging the flowers, cards embossed in gilt and pink. Chattering, clattering. Once, Peter ran all the way to Mexico to escape language.

I know The Sisters Three do not understand why I stopped going to see Daddy at Sunnydale. For a long while I had gone every day. But then they didn't witness his rectal, silken-latex lady-gloved finger of a lady doctor up his rectum, or hear his child-moan, though they have, I know, gone through as bad with him in different ways. But it was I who was blamed for the smuggled scotch (and rightly and proudly so). It was I who was sick unto death of begging for his Haldol, as if the drug which might have provided some relief from his nightmarish confusion were as filthy and illegal as smuggled-in cocaine.

They were enraged when I protested to a nurse about the constant sitting and resitting of my father at the lunch table. Every chair he sat down on someone else said was theirs. His slow, brittle glass-and-wire-and-porcelain journey down into that chair and the painful slow journey back up when yet another chair was again claimed. I told Head Nurse that my sense of Alzheimer's was it took all of the patient's concentration to perform a simple physical act such as sitting or even lying down and not once but four times my father had sat down, rigid with concentration, and four times been risen up like the Dead. "You shouldn't treat my father like that," I told her.

Head Nurse must have complained to The Sisters Three of my complaint, for Rachel lit into me as if it had been me who had raised the Un-Dead One in his slow painful journey.

"You didn't help one bit! You've made things worse for Daddy! Worse!" Rachel shouted at me.

I face my father, Timothy Glass, now, look down at him, white bone, white raft, frozen-white eyelashes sailing out, out beyond. . . .

Peter opens the door for Dinah, who is going into the corridor to talk to a nurse. I cannot really hear their voices very distinctly. My head is filled with a roaring. Daddy lies on his side, curled in a fetal position. Even now, dying, drifting in the dark turbulent coma seas between the high craggy cliffs of Alzheimer's, you can see the traces of a once-handsome man despite this ravaging disease.

His lips are slightly parted. One hand is tucked under his cheek. The other lies a little away from his face on the white, white hospital sheet. The pillowcase is sparkling white, white as snow, as eyelashes, and fluffed up as if his head were resting on a big fat white cloud and he were dreaming. And who is to say that he is not?

Tentatively I put my one hand over his that lies on the dazzling sheet. I close my fingers around his hand.

"Daddy," I say, "it's me, your Number-Two Daughter, the Dreamer."

And I know I do not imagine it. My Famous-Friend Doctor says such things are possible. My father's one eye opens slightly and slides towards me, Daughter Number-Two, his failure, his Dreamer. I can see the blue of his iris. I press my fingers harder against his hand. The slit of open eye remains open but does not look at anything, not me, the room, or the flowers. It just sits there, that one open blue slit, still as a glass eye.

"All our lives we ground together sidewise . . ." I begin. I want to say more but I cannot speak. I am crying, weeping great heaving sobs held inside me tight so that no one will hear. I do not want Daddy to hear my crying, his Dreamer. Or my sister. I want to tell Daddy everything about me that there is to tell.

I want to tell him, It is true all our lives we ground together sidewise. It will never be any different but I want to tell you it was worth the trip into your desert, into your War, into your opium dream, just to get to know you.

He will never again see summer. He, who so loved the earth, his Goddess, Rhea. This causes me as much pain as anything else in my life ever has. Peter comes up behind me and places his two hands on my heaving shoulders. He sees the open blue slit of my father's eye, still as glass, my fingers clenched over Daddy's hand.

"Didn't I tell you?"

Wordlessly, I nod. Only that. He does know. Something. Then I release my fingers from Timothy Glass's hand. My father. Daddy. I bunch a Kleenex in my hand and dab at my eyes and then turn to Dinah, who has just come back into the room. I say something about the flowers, how beautiful. Dinah smiles brightly and seems pleased. She says goodbye to Peter and me with a little wave.

I do not remember leaving Daddy's hospital room. I remember the twenty-four-hour daylight of the hospital corridors; electric sunshine. As long as the sun shines, death has no entrance, no Admittance Allowed.

I think of a phrase I've always remembered from an Audrey Thomas book, "When I was young and full of ragery."

Not so young any more but still filled with Ragery. Ragery at last for him and not against him.

After all these years.

The next thing I am conscious of is of being plunged into the dark bowels of the underground parking lot, the elevator doors sliding open. Bluebeard's castle, bloody corpses hanging from hooks, this castle of concrete and steel and black asphalt and tar. Glassed-in booths with men with bland faces in drab brown uniforms. Peter starts up the car engine. I light a cigarette and find I have to hold it between two hands, my hands are shaking so.

Peter lights a cigarette and we begin the drive up, up into the real sunlight, God's light.

Peter flashes his punched yellow ticket and we are out.

We do not talk much on the drive home. Peter leaves me to the quiet of my thoughts.

Peter hates to see anything die. If a wasp flies into his house he gently cups his hand behind it, cups it just behind the pointed black tail and urges it forward and out an open door or window without actually touching it. Once, there was a praying mantis trapped in his kitchen sink. He gently lifted the insect, one of the most extraordinary of insects with its beautiful pale-green body and praying hands, and he carried him out into the garden and set him on a dark-green leaf on the vine that covers one whole side of Peter's wooden fence.

I remember once I was sunning myself on the rocks in the little cove up at the cottage and turned to find a water moccasin lazing right beside me as peaceful and content as I was on the warm rocks in the sun. He sensed my movement and opened one cold grey eye. We eyed each other for moments, perhaps minutes. I did not blink. Or move. Nor did he. Obviously he had decided I was no threat to him. He knew somehow in that tiny reptilian brain that I, like he, wanted only the warmth of the glittering white and pink rocks and the sun. He closed his cold eye. And slept. I closed mine.

I do not know how long we lay there thus side by side, but I knew he would not harm me just as he knew I would not harm him. After a long while I picked up my damp towel and rose slowly, carefully, so as not to startle him, and soundlessly, on tiptoe, I walked away from the cove and the floating yellow water lilies and back to the cottage where we would spend the rest of the summer.

EPILOGUE

THE WHITE BLIND worms coil out, stretch, restless, searching in their dim pulsing.

Timothy remembers when he first kissed a girl. He was seven years old and rising from a pile of autumn leaves, all pear-yellow and crimson red and gold. He'd been lying there quite a long while daydreaming. He'd just read *A Connecticut Yankee in King Arthur's Court* by Mark Twain.

Oh, to be that crazy, lucky Yank. He loved Mark Twain. He'd read *Tom Sawyer* too. He liked the way Tom was always getting in trouble with that mean aunt of his but he had a good heart. He liked the way Tom was friends with Negroes because hardly anyone ever was. Not white people hardly ever anyway. Didn't that coloured fellow save Tom on the river raft? And him, he'd hardly ever seen a Negro. You didn't see many in Toronto.

And he'd never talked to one. Not really. Never even seen one right up close except that once, downtown outside Eaton's department store last Christmas. The Negro was selling warm chestnuts. Mother bought Timothy some. The man smiled at him and Timothy thanked the man and wished him a Merry Christmas. The Negro smiled again – such white, white teeth in all that deep dark-chocolate skin! – and wished him a Merry Christmas back. "Educated people say, 'Negro,'" Mother told him. But sometimes he forgot. He cupped the warm chestnuts like gold nuggets in his palm. He'd finally talked to a real live Negro just like Tom Sawyer did and the Negro had smiled at Tim and he'd smiled right back, right there on Queen Street.

Once, he'd even painted his whole face with dark-brown paint, the darkest brown paint he could find in his paint box, just to see if his teeth could look as white as that coloured man's had. But they didn't. He was disappointed. He had seldom seen a smile that looked as bright and real.

Daydreaming, daydreaming about Tom and laughing about Tom and that darn whitewashed fence and wishing he were that darn lucky Yank in King Arthur's Court. With eye-glasses. Heh, heh. The pile of autumn leaves was as warm as their gold and red colours. The sun warm, warm, a benediction. Then after a long while he opened his eyes and this little girl he was always watching, the one with the reddish-brown hair who lived two streets over in the poorer section of the neighbourhood but who he played with sometimes and watched *all* the time when she walked down his street, was just standing there staring at him. Just staring.

He'd always liked her. In fact, secretly, though he'd never tell a soul, he loved her. And he didn't know why, what made him do it, the heat of the sun of the day combined with the warmth of the leaves making him crazy, the daydreaming about Tom and Huck and the Yank and the gold nuggets in his hand, but he stood up quickly and suddenly kissed her right smack on the lips. Their teeth banged together he'd kissed her so hard on the lips. She hit him and whirled away in that little pink dress of hers – or was it blue? No, pink. She whirled away so fast he could see the white lace of her panties. He knew it was not gentlemanly to look at girls' underpanties but he did anyway.

And then she turned back for just a moment and smiled at him, a slow, kind of knowing smile much more grown-up than a five-year-old-girl smile and ran away real fast, pink dress flying. He touched his cheek where she had slapped him, more like a punch than a slap, and it felt warm, hot. He hoped it would stay hot forever.

Her name? It was Clare. Clara? No, it was Clarice. Clarice Magraw and he started dating her when she was in Grade Nine and he in Grade Ten. He took her to a high-school dance, the Christmas dance, and she was dressed up beautiful in a green velvet dress, her silk stockings on those gorgeous legs, and he gave her a corsage with dark-green leaves and tiny red Christmas mistletoe berries sprouting from the green. She slipped on the ice in the high-school parking lot and he grabbed her by her long brown hair to keep her from falling. Just as he grabbed her hair, Clarice a-sprawling, the headlights of a car swung in and beamed right in on both of them, a spotlight on her humiliation. She said she could have killed him. She hardly looked at him all night, let alone danced with him.

Boy, that Clarice. She was something. A beauty. A real beauty. Sometimes in the summer he took her up to his parents' summer house by the lake and once she caught a huge trout, all silver and speckled brown. Beautiful, shapely legs in that blue bathing suit of hers.

He frowns deep in the Place of Not. The huge white worms stir, restless, pulsing dimly. He remembers, when he was five, Father took him to a building filled with children made of poorly stitched-together rags. But he respected his father. Boys do. Boys should. Sometimes during the Depression there were only potatoes in the house to eat for dinner. And Father gambled. Sometimes it made Mother weep and that made Timothy mad! So mad! Sometimes he gambled away nearly all their money.

Timothy remembers once, when he was six, Father begging Mother for her emerald and sapphire and diamond rings and opal and pearl necklace to pawn just until he could get the money to buy them back, he swore. Mother refused and Timothy was glad, glad! Don't give him a darn thing! Not one darn thing! Then he clapped his hand hard over his mouth, afraid he'd said it out loud, and he went and hid for two hours in the dumbwaiter that ran between the four floors of their house, just in case Father had heard him say it out loud. Hid there so that if Father had heard he would not find him. Would not find him and put him in the Home for the Children Made of Rags that he'd once taken him to.

He remembers dim green corridors, long dark shadows, tiny high windows, terrible smells, and screaming, awful, awful screaming. The word *monster* coils like smoke in his mind. Then he feels ashamed. He respected Father, always. Boys do. He loved Mother.

He remembers talking to someone with snow-white hair just like Mother's about Father, after he'd shown her a photograph of Father. The woman – girl? – but he cannot remember who she was or if she were grown, a woman or a girl, but she said his father looked stern. He laughed a short laugh, like a punctuation mark, and said he was. That. Stern. Who was she? Who else did he know with snow-white hair like Mother? It seems to him that whoever this woman or girl was, she was young with her snow-white hair just like Mother was young with hers.

Snow-white eyelashes.

But he can't remember her. Who she was. What her name was. He supposes it isn't important.

One Christmas he got a hand-carved coach which had hand-carved wooden horses with small leather saddles drawing their coach by real tiny leather reins, and the coach was lit up inside with little red light bulbs. Miniature wood-carved people sat in the coach. Men and women. Women in little blue velvet hats. Men in little black satin high-top hats. How old was he? Nine?

His mind hopscotches. He remembers being two years old and just walking, following his older sister Kate everywhere. He came after her on his chubby little legs and she picked him up and swung him up high and he laughed and laughed.

Kate was fourteen years older than he was. His older brother Budd was nearly nineteen years older. He loves Kate. She said when he was a little boy just before he went off that first summer to the farm that she thought he was "the bee's knees."

The bee's knees! Sister Kate said that of him. Sister Kate loves him. He loves her. Kate is beautiful, tall, statuesque, with a lovely, slender figure. Curls piled high atop her proud head. She has a noble neck. A pale-white throat. The neck and throat of an aristocrat, a born lady.

He remembers the red velvet curtains in the dining room and the solid-gold dinner bell. The bell clanged and the clapper was pulled by a gold velvet cord.

He is five years old and eating in the dining room, the red velvet drapes drawn around the huge dark-oak dining table. It is his last night home before he goes up north to the farm to "toughen him up" because he is a sickly child. He knows he is sickly and is ashamed of it. He is a little afraid of going so far, far from home, far away from Sister Kate and Mother. Not Father. But he respects Father. Boys should. Boys do. He is a little excited too. It might be an adventure like Tom Sawyer's adventure.

Father said, "Use your butter fork when taking a ball of butter from the butter dish."

"Yes, sir."

Kate leans forward and says, "Are you excited, Timmy?"

"Kind of," he says.

"Are you a little worried, anxious, dear, about going away?" Mother asks.

"Of course not," Father says. "Why should he be? He's a big boy. It will toughen him. Make him strong. Remember, Timothy Glass, that farmer said you must work hard, pull your own weight, son."

"Yes, Father."

Kate laughed. Her laughter like a tinkling, burbling waterfall. "I bet you'll have a wonderful time, Timmy. All those farm animals. Pigs and cows and chickens, maybe dogs and, of course, horses."

"He's there to work. To be made tough," Father says.

"Yes, sir."

Kate smiles across the table at him. Mother lays her soft-skinned hand over his. Her rings sparkle under the Tiffany lamp hanging above the table. Father eats his roast beef, and asks in French for the butter dish to be passed. *"Voulez-vous passer du beurre, s'il vous plaît?"*

Already both Father and Mother are teaching him French and Latin.

Timothy passes the butter, careful to include the little sterling-silver butter fork on the bone-china dish with the perfectly round butter balls.

The rest of the dinner is eaten in silence.

Mother took him up early the next morning by train to the farm. One of the hired men picked them up at the train station. Mother leans her cheek down for a kiss and Timothy grabs her hard and fast around the neck and kisses her hard on her sweet-smelling powdered cheek. Mother always smelled sweet as ripe plums with her powder and perfume and rose water. She pats him on the arm. "It will be just fine, dear. Now go with the hired man. I will write to you and to the farmer, Mr. Ned Fraser, once a week to see how you are getting along. I've packed envelopes addressed home with stamps so that you can write to me. And Sister Kate." A pause. "Father, too, of course." Another shorter pause. "Remember to be respectful always. Call him Mr. Fraser. Now go, get on with you. That's a boy." He turns away from Mother.

The hired man bends to take his two suitcases but Timothy only lets him take one, announcing, "Sir, I can manage this one fine." Once he is in the hired man's truck he has a deep aching feeling and an urge to look back at Mother waiting for the next train to take her home but he does not. He remembers for a long time as they drive down the dusty, rutted roads the smell of Mother's powdered cheek, her rose water. Sweet as ripe plums. There are fir trees, tall scraggly trees reaching spidery grey fingers into the blue, blue sky. Yellow mustard fields that wave in golden blankets, gold oceans. Wild weeds and wildflowers grow beside the roads, gnarled bushes. For a long time they ride in silence. Then the hired man says, "We're nearly there. Your name is Timothy?"

"Yes, sir."

"Timothy Glass, the sickly lad."

"Yes, sir." His cheeks flame.

The hired hand laughs suddenly and sticks out a hand brown with sun and dirt and says, "I'll call you Tim if you call me Bill."

"Yes, sir. Bill, I mean." Timothy shakes his hand.

"Ever smoke, boy?"

"You mean cigarettes, sir – Bill?"

"Yeah, a cigarette, sure."

"No, gosh no."

"Well, I'd bet surer than hell that'll change soon enough." And Bill laughed a big, deep laugh.

Timothy sat back against the dusty seat of the truck. He relaxed for the first time. This was going to be all right, this was going to be just fine. It was going to be an adventure just like Tom Sawyer's. Bill said he would have a smoke soon and Bill had a rich, deep laugh.

"This is all ours," Bill says, turning off the engine, his hand giving a wide sweep of what seems to Timothy like a thousand-acre farm. There are ragged old yellow dogs in the farmyard with bits of ears and tails missing. Chickens strut here and there pecking at the dusty ground. There are cats of all kinds, black cats and grey cats and striped tabby cats and white fluffy cats. Scrawny cats and fat cats lay curled in the sun or on the wide farmhouse verandah. "Most of them cats live in the barn but they're real good to have. Natural-born predators. Kill off all the mice and any rats when they dare come. Male and female both got balls. 'Scuse my language again. I forget you're just a little boy and a highbrow at that."

Timothy takes offence at "little boy" and "highbrow" so he says, "Oh, I'm not so little. Father says I'm a big boy. And I'm real used to cuss words. Use them sometimes myself even." He tries to puff out his chest to look bigger, older.

"You do, eh? Good, no problem at the farm with you then. Most of the dogs live in the bunkhouse, three always in the yard, constant watchers, and five of them, mangy things, live in the farmhouse with the mister and missus. The missus's name's Flora. The dogs are real good guards, natural protectors of man. Man's best friend and that's the truth."

"Four cats just, live in the house. Horatio, Mandy, Flo, after Flora, and Ned, named after Mr. Ned. Flora's a good woman and a damn good cook. She'll fatten you up, you better believe." Bill poked him in his scrawny ribcage. "Gotta fatten you up a little before I take you out behind the barn for your first smoke so you won't die on me, coughing yourself to death." Bill laughed.

"Oh, I won't die," Timothy says bravely, not quite sure that he won't.

Bill gives him a narrow-eyed look. Bill has hazel eyes. "I bet you wouldn't either, boy. Now I'll take you into the house to meet the mister and missus of the place."

When they get out of the truck Timothy insists on carrying both his suitcases though they nearly drag him down onto his knees into the dusty yard along with the dogs and the cats and the pecking dirty-white chickens.

Walking, almost crawling behind Bill, he sees the gleam of a glass whiskey flask in Bill's back pocket. A small one. Timothy knows what whiskey is. And port. Father has a glass of port every night with dinner. And two glasses of whiskey before bed every night. But Father's whiskey bottles look a lot more expensive. Father's whiskey bottles have gold silk tassels around the neck. Timothy thinks if he ever drinks whiskey he'll drink Bill's kind.

Flora is plain and plump as an old log but kind, gentle, joking. Mr. Fraser sticks out a massive hand and says, "Forget the mister, boy, call me Ned. All my hands do and you're one of my hands, right?"

"Right, sir," Timothy says, his small hand lost and crushed in Mr. Ned's huge, meaty one.

"And her," Mr. Ned Fraser says with a nod to his wife, who is at the woodstove cooking up wonderful-smelling things. "Call her Flora. Right, Flo?"

With a nod to Timothy. "Of course, dear, Flora it is."

She is busy all the while walking back and forth with steaming pans and pot holders, aprons and skirts swishing.

Bill says, "Hey, Ned, better take a picture of the boy now so we can send it home to his mother, a real decent lady. After all, it's the cleanest he'll ever be until he leaves here."

Ned laughs and so do the two other hired men who are sitting in the kitchen, their chairs tilted back on two legs, smoking cigarettes they've rolled by hand. Timothy stares, fascinated. Father smokes a pipe. The occasional cigar.

Mr. Ned Fraser himself takes Timothy down to the fence by the mustard field and has him perch on it. Timothy is wearing what his mother thought were suitable farm clothes. Freshly laundered and starched blue overalls, a clean white short-sleeved shirt, and a straw boater with a blue ribbon around it.

"Smile, Timmy," Mr. Ned Fraser says.

And Timothy does, and although it is a shy smile it is a real smile, for he can't wait to have his first smoke out behind the barn or eat Flora's dinner. He's seen the whiskey flask tucked into Bill's back pocket. He's never seen such a big chest as the one on Mr. Ned, a barrel chest more power-ful-looking than he's seen even in pictures of prizefighters in newspapers, but you can tell there's something wrong with his legs. They're short and kind of drag behind him when he walks.

This is going to be as good as Tom Sawyer's and Huck Finn's adventures, maybe even better.

His smile broadens.

This is going to be swell.

Behind him a field of mustard quivers in waves, a golden ocean.

The camera shutter falls.

Clicks.

He spent the next thirteen summers working the farm and again every fall to help with the final harvesting on Labour Day. Thirteen summers of working with the hired men, haying and mowing and pulling tree stumps and rocks from the fields and planting and mowing and watering and feeding those damn stupid chickens. So stupid that when they fell off their perch you had to pick them up and put them back up on it. Chickens had no sense at all. He had helped gather eggs. Ploughed the fields with the work-horses, the drays, planted mustard seeds. He shovelled coal into the coal-bin. Chopped wood. He did the hundred other things there were to do on a farm.

Sometimes Flora or Ned had him or one of the other hands behead a couple of the chickens and she'd roast them for dinner. He never liked that part much; killing the thing even if it was stupid. Flora was a good cook and all the meals were huge and delicious but his favourite meal on the farm right from that first year when he was five was breakfast.

There were rashers and rashers of bacon and eggs, fried over-easy and sunny-side up, fried potatoes and fried green tomatoes, milk fresh-squeezed from the cow's teat that early morn, jugs of juice and apples and plums and pears in thick blue bowls, steaming hot pots of black coffee and pots of rich tea, buttered rolls, dough freshly rolled by Flora before sun-up, and sausages spitting in the pan, plates of toast piled sky-high and sweet potato pie, with marshmallows. And when Tim, as the hired men had all come to call him that first year at five years old, settled back after breakfast on his chair, the hands rolled up and lit their smokes and chawed their tobacco.

He didn't get his first smoke out behind the barn until he was seven; his first drink from a whiskey flask until he was eight. His first friend there besides Bill was Old Bob. Old Bob was a dapple-grey horse. Old Bob was his best friend in the world.

In the afternoons, the hired hands would be sweating and filthy, and one of the them would yell, "Hey, sun's high up in the sky and three o'clock and time for the swim hole!"

Old Bob, faithful as the dogs who ran yelping with joy after the men down to the swim hole, would follow along, Tim riding Old Bob's swayed grey back, his arms cradling his beloved friend's neck. At the swim hole the men and Tim and Old Bob all swam bare-ass, Tim jumping off Old Bob's back. Again and again he dove from Old Bob's back, and swung from his neck laughing, sputtering as the horse playfully ducked him beneath the water.

Sometimes at night he'd slip out to the barn where Old Bob slept and sneak him carrots and sugar cubes. Other times he'd sneak him a snort of whiskey, which Old Bob liked as well as anyone else on the farm. Some nights he slept for a while curled on top of Old Bob's back or around his mottled hooves in the straw before he roused himself and went back to the bunkhouse.

On cold nights, and it could get cold at night up north, even in summer, Tim would cover Old Bob with his scratchy grey blanket for warmth.

And Tim did toughen up. By the time he was seven, he was healthy and more muscled than any other boy his age back home. He grew strong and tall, six foot one and a half by the time he was fifteen. Father no longer gave him disparaging looks over his newspaper, followed by his long sigh, the newspaper rustling as if the newspaper itself were angry.

He sat with the hired men in the bunkhouse at night as they drank and smoked and played cards and jawed. Some of the hands had pin-ups of movie stars on the bunkhouse walls. Tim had books. But the jawing was how he found out the man he had come to love and call Uncle Ned had come to have such a powerfully built chest and arms.

"Oh, Mr. Ned, didn't you know, boy?" one of the hands, Sam, said to Tim when Tim was eight. "Mr. Ned had polio when he was nine or ten thereabouts. That can kill you, let alone cripple you, but you know Mr. Ned. He refused to die. He refused to be a cripple. Story has it he dragged himself from room to room in his house, up and down stairs for years just by his arms, and crawled on his chest and belly like a snake. Learned to lift weights lying there on his back. But I never saw a man more powerfully built in the arms or chest." Sam looked over at the other hands for confirmation. "Have any of you boys?"

No, they all solemnly shook their heads, *no*.

"Not even prizefighters like in the newspapers," Tim said, remembering his first impression of Uncle Ned.

Tim and the hands went back to playing cards. Betting for toothpicks to pick their teeth with, tobacco and whiskey. Tim saved half the whiskey he won at cards for Old Bob.

The long white worms sigh, curl into balls, uncurl again white as cold moons, white as old bones.

Something flashes briefly in Timothy Glass's mind. He remembers King Street in winter and people scurrying through the falling snow looking like ghosts; perhaps they are ghosts. He sees a banner above a makeshift desk right outside in the middle of the street, a banner with print on it in black lettering: RECRUITING CENTRE.

War.

1940.

He sees something suddenly, a bright, quick flash like a lightning bolt. A young airman, come home, Fly Boy cap jauntily resting on his head, is kneeling down on the ground and kissing the good earth. The good, solid earth of home.

He shivers in the deep dark grotto in the Place of Not.

He feels bats' wings stretching out over his face and covering it in a mourning shroud, the wings dark as night, as Death. Their webbed wings like black autumn leaves.

Timothy Glass is confused, frightened. Where is he? What is this deep, deep place where air doesn't even skim over his skin? Where are the hired hands? Bill, Sam. The other hands. Uncle Ned and Aunt Flora?

Where is Old Bob?

"So, Mr. T. Glass," the nurse says softly, "you're still with us after all."

Tim is running through a field of shimmering mustard with Old Bob, both of them are laughing, laughing. Finally they stop under a tree in the apple orchard past the mustard field, the field an ocean of gold, the desert a shivering hot-white ocean – *What?* No matter. He must have read that in a book somewhere. Dickens? Thackeray? Stendhal? Somewhere. He gives Old Bob an apple. Old Bob eats it greedily, gratefully. He bids the horse lie down. The old horse settles his old bones down in the orchard beside Tim among swollen fallen apples. Together they gorge themselves on apples. Tim is sixteen. He is telling Old Bob secrets as he has done since he first met him all those years ago.

"Horses are really smart and you're smarter than most so you can understand why I love her so. I told you how beautiful she is, those long legs, shapely and gorgeous though not as long as yours, Bob ol' boy. She needs protecting. Someone to protect her. I think we'll get engaged when we graduate from high school. Then, like I told you, I'm going to study architecture. Build houses. My houses will be miracles."

He is lying blissfully in a gold and crimson-red pile of warm autumn leaves. A little girl kisses him. Or he her? Who is that little girl? He sees her panties and blushes as she twirls away on a cloud. It is not gentlemanly to look, but he looks anyway. He wants to call out after the cloud, the twirling girl with white lace frosting on her panties, *Wait!* but the cloud becomes murky, vaporous mist.

He is lying in a sun-warmed pile of gold and scarlet-red and pear-yellow autumn leaves.

Parrots' wings in all the colours of dusk and twilight and tall glasses of bright lemonade fall like dust in the desert heat in the tents of the Arabs.

What?

He is confused.

Old Bob?

Now he remembers, remembers it all.

It is his thirteenth summer up at the farm. He is eighteen years old. He and all the hands are there, Sam and Bill and Harry, Old John, and Uncle Ned. Aunt Flora is in the kitchen.

Doing – something . . .

The hired hands and Timothy are drawing straws. Twelve long straws, one short straw. Thirteen hired hands. The short straw loses. Uncle Ned oversees the proceedings, his dark, almost opaque grey eyes are narrowed. He is thinking. His barrel chest breathes in-out, his powerful arms are wrapped around his massive chest.

Clocks had clocks. One smack in the centre of his fore-head for . . . for . . . which time? A gold watch fob. Which time? There was so much time he had to account for.

He remembers a girl named Isadora Wind.

She was dressed all in blue and had wings of silk.

He wonders if he loved her.

He thinks he did.

He remembers someone else, Clare? Clara?

He thinks of wolves howling, calling out from high angry crags.

He hears the parrots screaming in the black sea, in the dark night.

He feels a tiny monkey's hands wrapped tight around his neck, the sea dense as crushed black velvet. Suffocating.

Timothy hears mournful sounds. A singing that is a weep-ing, a dirge. *We are poor little lambs who have lost our way. . . .*

The dogs, the cats . . . the Fly Boys drowned. . . .

One parrot went mad the second time they crashed into the sea.

He remembers a girl, a child with snow-white hair and snow-white eyelashes like Mother.

Who?

He cannot remember who she was, only that she was.

The parrots' feathers in all the colours of dusk and twi-light fall like dust under the hot-white desert sun.

Opium pipes.

There were blood-red sandstorms.

Timothy draws the short straw.

After a silent supper, during which no one could eat, Timothy went to the bunkhouse and picked up the revolver that Uncle Ned had given him before supper, when Uncle Ned had gripped his hand.

Timothy put four bullets into it.

The Fly Boys kept the mad parrot as long as they could reasonably do so. All day and night the parrot babbled, swung around and around on his perch like a crazed Ferris wheel, saying over and over, "Good boy, pretty boy, Othello. Good, good pretty boy." He screamed it, babbling it night and day and revolving round and round on his perch non-stop. "This poor bugger's gone insane," Ian Glass said. "It isn't right. He's in agony." The parrot, who was named Othello jointly by Timothy and Ian, was put out of his misery.

Ian Glass wrung Othello's neck.

"It's kindest. Birds' bones snap easily."

Ian dead on the white jagged Rock in '42.

Best damn friend in the whole damn War, best damn friend in the whole damn world.

You're in the army now, ya can scream and shout, ya'll never get out, you're in the army now!

Uncle Ned said it had to be done. They drew straws. Fair is fair. Uncle Ned said that Old Bob had, years ago, lived past any usefulness to the farm. Uncle Ned said, "Old Bob is nothing but ancient old bones dragging around the farmyard, sleeping in his stall half the time. He has to be — put to rest." Timothy blinked back the tears rising under his eyelids but made no protest. It was the way things were done on a farm when an animal outlived its usefulness. It had always been the way. Uncle Ned barely scraped a living together from his farm. The first three years Timothy was there Uncle Ned could not pay hands at all, just bare wages from then on. He had been more than fair when it came to Old Bob, Tim knew. It was a small working farm and susceptible to seasons. Drought. Rain. Rising rivers. Cold. It had always been so with old, useless farm animals.

Shot.

Timothy checked the revolver once more before going out to the barn, to Old Bob. Four bullets. The revolver was sleek and black as oil.

Timothy in the grotto remembers suddenly a sea as dark black and sleek as oil. A killing sea.

But Old Bob, the barn, Old Bob.

He has to go there and do it.

He drew the short straw.

In the dark night Timothy leaves the bunkhouse, the revolver in his hand cold as death despite the heat of his palm, death pulsing beneath his skin. Under our skins lies death. Death lies under his skin tonight, in his warm palm, the revolver cooling it. He will pull the trigger. Four bullets. His fingers run over the chamber. He walks from the bunkhouse, past Uncle Ned's and Aunt Flora's farmhouse, and through the farmyard towards the barn.

He hears parrots screaming, babbling somewhere far-off.

The gun sleek and black as oil, black as a killing sea.

The Fly Boys sang to keep up their courage as they treaded water hour after hour as it grew dark. And cold.

Animals and birds died, men died. They were all just boys killing boys.

Timothy walks on towards Old Bob, towards the barn, the stall, Old Bob.

When he reaches the barn he opens the door softly as he always does, lest he disturb Old Bob's sleep. But Old Bob is not sleeping; he is awake and standing in his stall, nuzzling on some hay, chewing it slowly, thoughtfully. He looks up at his beloved friend and gives a whinny of sheer pleasure.

"Hey, Bob," Timothy whispers. "Old Bob, good ol' thing."

He approaches Old Bob on soft feet, quiet, quiet. Old Bob pricks his ears forward, happily awaiting the cube of sugar, the carrot stick, cupped in Timothy's palm. He always gets one or the other. Sometimes both. Occasionally some whiskey.

"Hey, Bob, Old Bob, old friend," Timothy whispers, soft, hot tears under his eyelids. Old Bob looks at him adoringly from his big liquid-brown eyes. Doe eyes. Deer-caught. Timothy thinks of camels' eyes. Loving, deep-brown eyes, Old Bob.

"Hey, Bob, Old Bob."

Then Timothy shoots Old Bob once between those trusting dark eyes. The first bullet doesn't take.

That was the hell of it, Timothy will remember all of his life Old Bob's surprised brown eyes looking square into his own blue ones. The eyes disbelieving but still filled with trust and love. That made it all far worse. Timothy cocks the gun again. The second bullet hits square between the loving eyes. It takes. Old Bob gives a strange, wounded moan, more human than animal, and topples over onto his side in his stall. Two bullet holes between his trusting eyes pour a red river.

Timothy blinks. Sets the sleek black revolver down on the barn floor. Then goes into Old Bob's stall and cradles the old beast's bloody head in his lap. His work jeans are covered in blood. Carefully he lays Old Bob's head down. His hands have Old Bob's blood on them. He does not wipe his hands clean on the straw. He leaves Old Bob's blood glowing, gleaming there in his palms. He covers Old Bob with the grey blanket Old Bob was so fond of on cold nights and that Timothy always covered him with when there was a chill in the air. Gently, he draws the scratchy grey blanket up around Old Bob's dappled-grey, now red-stained neck. He places one hand on his old friend's fine long muzzle. He strokes his old mottled hooves.

Timothy draws the blanket up over Old Bob's head, his unseeing liquid-brown eyes.

He leaves Old Bob then, closing the stall door behind him. To keep him warm. Timothy picks the black revolver up off the barn floor. It lies cold in his palm. Quietly he leaves the barn, pulling the door shut. Keep the cold out, gets damn cold up here, even in summer.

And then he is running, running, the revolver in his bloody hand.

He sees a white sign with black lettering on it fluttering in the wind.

He does not understand. He runs.

He runs through the farmyard, out past the mustard fields, runs and runs. Runs out past the work fields and on past the orchard. Runs until his breath is bursting his lungs, the pain tearing his chest apart and him welcoming it. He runs on and on past the plum patch and finally down to the old swim hole where he does not stop running not even at water's edge where, running still, he flings the gun with a mighty sweep of his arm into the swim hole and keeps on running into the water runs until the water is knee deep, thigh deep, waist deep, chest deep, neck deep, where he throws back his head and howls and weeps under a moon as shiny and cold and hard as a dime.

Timothy Glass scoffs at God.

Timothy Glass rails against God.

Timothy wants God.

Baa, baa, baa . . .

Acknowledgements

I should first like to thank Dr. Mark Teplitsky, who, aside from the usual touchstoning he always affords me, was most helpful with certain medical-technical matters for this book. I put to him lots of questions on the possibility of, and the nature of, a "mind existence" in non-sentient states. Any conclusions I have drawn are solely my own.

Next, a thanks to Dean Cooke. At last, at long last, an agent who was not only willing to take a look at my work, but was prepared to represent me. And represent me well he has. Sorry about the frantic phone calls.

And a huge thanks to my editor, Ellen Seligman. Working with her has been a dream. A bonding of sorts I believe has taken place through, not least of all, our mutual love of all creatures. Especially pussycats.

A thank you also to the Canada Arts Council, whose grant the year previous helped dull the fangs of the wolves nipping at the back of my sweater.

Patricia Ridenour

Margaret Gibson received instant acclaim on the publication of her award-winning first collection of short stories, *The Butterfly Ward* (1976). One of the stories from the collection, "Making It," was made into the now-classic movie *Outrageous*, starring Craig Russell; another story, "Ada," was made into a CBC-TV movie, directed by Claude Jutra. The story of her own custody battle for her son was made into the TV movie *For the Love of Aaron*. She has since published four acclaimed short-story collections: *Considering Her Condition* (1978); *Sweet Poison* (1993); *The Fear Room and Other Stories* (1996); and *Desert Thirst* (1997).

Opium Dreams, her first novel, won the Chapters/ Books in Canada First Novel Award in 1998, and has been published in translation in Germany.

Margaret Gibson lives in Toronto, where she is at work on her next novel.